New Fiction

WRITING CHALLENGE SERIES: CANDYFLOSS CLOUDS

Edited by

Sarah Andrew

First published in Great Britain in 2003 by
NEW FICTION
Remus House,
Coltsfoot Drive,
Peterborough, PE2 9JX
Telephone (01733) 898101
Fax (01733) 313524

SB ISBN 1 85929 071 X

FOREWORD

When 'New Fiction' ceased publishing there was much wailing and gnashing of teeth, the showcase for the short story had offered an opportunity for practitioners of the craft to demonstrate their talent.

Bringing in a new side to New Fiction, we introduced the Writing Challenge Series. One paragraph and numerous endings to show imagination and creativity.

The art of the short story writer has been practised from ancient days, with many gifted writers producing small, but hauntingly memorable stories that linger in the imagination.

I believe this selection of stories will leave echoes in your mind for many days. Read on and enjoy the pleasure of that most perfect form of literature, the short story.

Parvus Est Bellus.

CONTENTS

PHILANTHROPY
Anne Rolfe-Brooker

Candyfloss clouds were the only interruption in the bright blue sky. Beneath them was the hustle and bustle of everyday life carrying on regardless. People always found a way of ignoring the bad things that were happening and sometimes the good things as well. The city was buzzing; it was a bank holiday. Practically everybody had the day off work. The children dragged their parents around the shops trying to squeeze extra gifts out of them, and the elderly took time to sit on park benches and let the breeze blow them down memory lane. It was a day when anything could happen and anything was possible.

The sun beat down hot and hungry on the sunbathers in the city park, negating the sparse shade provided by the tall, thirsty trees that stood, sentinels of time, above the neatly cut grass.

Slowly, imperceptibly, a soft breeze covered the heat-baked pavements and the shadows lengthened in the park as late afternoon gave way, reluctantly, to early evening.

The jammed streets and the packed shops all emptied, diverse humanity scattered back to their homes, leaving a strange stillness, an atmosphere of abandonment, punctuated only occasionally by the passing snuffle of a car's engine or the far barking of a dog.

John Travis stepped outside his antique shop and turned to lock the door.

He was a small, balding, bespectacled man with dark, luminous eyes framed by laughter lines. His grey silk suit was bespoke and his shoes finest Italian leather. Nothing about John Travis was shoddy.

He began to walk towards the car park where his silver Mercedes shouted to be noticed among the few BMWs and Volvos, whose owners were probably working late.

A gnarled hand suddenly shot out in front of his face and a voice, dry as a fallen autumn leaf said, 'Money for food Guv? Give us money for food.'

John's eyes travelled the length of the outstretched arm and he found himself looking at an elderly tramp dressed in baggy trousers, an old worn lumberjack's shirt, the whole ensemble covered by an oily raincoat, that at one time may have been fawn coloured. The face that peered back at him was weather-beaten, but pleasant, the blue eyes twinkling with a light that seemed to dance within them and a grey beard that defied the rules of gravity by growing all ways at once.

John pulled out some coins from his side pocket where he kept his small change and after a cursory glance at the money, flipped four pound coins into the still-patient hand in front of him.

The gentleman of the road looked at the donation and smiled a slow smile that lit up his face and suffused his whispery voice with a peculiar warmth.

'A pound a wish, Guv, for your generosity - a pound a wish.'

John smiled back. 'Don't mention it,' he said, 'I've been down on my luck myself.' He walked on, thinking to himself, but never so down as you, old man.

As he approached his car, he felt sure that the tramp was now making his way to the nearest pub, but he turned anyway to maybe wave goodbye to him. There was nobody in sight.

As he slid into the upholstered leather driver's seat, a youth appeared at his window and tapped on the glass. John pressed the automatic window winder and the glass slid gently to half mast.

'You know what I think about old gits like you with cars like this?' the red-haired youth, obviously somewhat inebriated, enquired, his demeanour announcing the fact that he did not really care what John knew about his mind's innermost workings.

'Would you mind stepping away from the car, please. I'm trying to go home,' John said quietly.

'Oh, la de da then,' returned the teenage menace. 'Oh, would I mind? Yes I would bloody mind, and I s'pose your home is a bloody mansion too!' he said belligerently.

'No, actually it's not. Now please stand aside,' John said quietly and gently turned the ignition key. The engine purred into readiness.

The youth leaned against the car door and lowered his face towards John's. 'I wish your lot would all drop dead,' he said, almost confidentially.

'And I wish you would go to Hell,' John replied, almost conversationally.

There was a sudden flash, a scream, and an overwhelming smell of sulphur and John became aware of the fact that the annoying presence at the side of his car had vanished, apparently into thin air.

The unexpectedness of the whole thing left him trembling, this time with shock more than anger, and as he sat waiting for his nerves to steady and to assure himself that he had not imagined the whole thing, a quiet, still voice in his head echoed; 'A pound a wish, Guv, for your generosity - a pound a wish.'

'In that case,' John muttered darkly to himself, 'I wish I had a damned large whiskey.'

He realised with some alarm that a brimming tumbler of the amber nectar was being pushed by an unseen force into his left hand, which still gripped the steering wheel. Not particularly caring at this point where it had come from, nor from whom, he paused briefly to satisfy himself that it was, indeed, whiskey and downed it in five large gulps.

He closed his eyes, and lay back in the car seat, his faith in reality completely shattered, only to have his reverie interrupted by a hand tapping his shoulder through the open car window.

'Good evening sir - may I see your driver's licence, if you please?'

John opened his eyes in horror at the vision now standing beside his car. It was dressed in the blue uniform of Her Majesty's Metropolitan Police and it did not look particularly pleased to see him sitting in the driving seat of a brand new silver Mercedes with an empty whisky tumbler in his hand.

'Good evening officer, it's not what it seems . . .' he began inadequately, searching his mind frantically for a logical explanation.

'That's what they all say, sir, that's what they all say. Now if I could see your driver's licence and then perhaps you wouldn't mind coming to the station with me for an assessment of your alcohol level, although judging by what I've just seen, I'd say that was pretty unnecessary, wouldn't you sir?'

John tried half-heartedly to laugh, his soul in reality sinking beneath the realisation that he was about to be arrested for drink driving.

'Would you mind turning off your engine, sir?' the policeman asked good naturedly, 'we don't want you making a getaway in your condition, do we?'

John turned off the engine and started searching his pockets for his wallet. Then he remembered that he had put it on the desk in the antique shop, while telephoning a business acquaintance, having taken it out to retrieve the card with the relevant number, and had forgotten to pick it up on his way out.

'I'm afraid officer, that I've left it behind . . . in the shop . . . Travis Antiques,' he stuttered, again realising that things were going from bad to worse.

The officer reached into his breast pocket and took out his notebook. He was beginning to read John his rights, when that small, paper thin voice whispered in his head, 'A pound a wish, Guv- for your generosity, a pound a wish.'

'I wish you'd go away and leave me alone,' John said tentatively, not sure that the officer would succumb to what he now firmly believed was his own personal psychic experience.

The officer put away his notebook and smiled at him. 'Have a pleasant evening, Sir,' he said. 'Nice car.'

With that he touched his cap and wandered off towards the park, happily humming Men of Harlech to himself.

John let out a sigh of relief and considered the options open to him. He was now convinced he had met a gentleman of the road who, for some unknown reason, had chosen him to be the recipient of four wishes which the Fates, for whatever reason of their own, chose to grant him.

So far he had used three of his wishes, albeit unwisely, and he now sat and contemplated the possibilities before him. He could wish for wealth, of course, but he was already well-off, and he had always considered too much money might be something of a burden rather than a blessing. In most stories wish recipients also asked for health, but he was reminded of a maiden aunt of his who had lived until she was 104 and her last days were beset with tribulations, not least of which was her keen belief that the world had gone to Hell since her youth, leading to a continuous sense of frustration, which she took out on anybody who went near her, making their lives nearly as damned miserable as hers.

He could always wish for a harem of beautiful women, but would the wish to be able to keep up with them count as two wishes, or would the two go together he wondered? It would be no use having a harem if all he could do was look at them. Besides, his wife would certainly object, and his dog didn't like strangers in the house.

That didn't leave an awful lot to wish for really, and he sat for some twenty minutes, cursing fate for the dilemma in which he currently found himself.

As in the case of the Buddha, enlightenment was swift and complete. Hew got out of the car, locked the doors with the button on his keychain and walked swiftly back towards his shop. Letting himself in, he picked up his wallet and paused at the door. 'I wish everything was as it was before,' he said aloud, and straightening his tie, John Travis stepped outside his antique shop and locked the door.

He looked left and right before venturing onto the pavement, then started walking towards the car park. In the middle distance a figure was walking towards him, but a close scrutiny enabled him to see that it was not the old tramp. He walked on, lost in thought wondering if he had dreamed the whole thing. The streets were almost empty, and he felt suddenly vulnerable and alone.

As he reached the spot where he had encountered the old man, the solitary figure which had been ahead of him, drew level. He looked and saw that it was a bag lady, with smiling blue eyes and life-lined face. She was dressed in a long, dowdy, tartan dress, her feet encased in men's workboots, the laces trailing miserably behind the uppers.

She thrust out a thin, hungry hand in front of him. 'Money for good, Guv? Give us money for food.'

John let out a wild scream and looked at her with horror, his whole body frozen with unbelievable fear.

She held her hand closer to his face, and looked at him with sorrow in her eyes. Yet just beyond the sorrow, John could sense the laughter. 'Not on your bloody life, woman!' he said vehemently, and with a supreme effort of will, turned away from her and began running towards the car park.

FLIGHT OF FANCY
Joan Strong

Candyfloss clouds were the only interruption in the bright blue sky. Beneath them was the hustle and bustle of everyday life carrying on regardless. People always found a way of ignoring the bad things that were happening and sometimes the good things as well. The city was buzzing; it was a bank holiday. Practically everybody had the day off work. The children dragged their parents around the shops trying to squeeze extra gifts out of them, and the elderly took time to sit on park benches and let the breeze blow them down memory lane. It was a day when anything could happen and anything was possible.

Anything was possible when Pearl was about; there was no sitting down on park benches for her and Alf that day. They arrived at the Jubilee fête and flower show in Victoria Park long after its official opening by the Mayor, Alf trudging behind his wife, making much use of his stout walking stick.

His voice carried a note of complaint as he called out to her, 'Hold on Pearl, what's the rush?'

She barely glanced round at him as she replied, 'I told you this morning - the balloons.'

'You what?' Alf stopped short and, short of breath, leaned on his stick.

Just visible over the crowns of the oak trees that separated the park from the recreation ground loomed the domes of two enormous and colourful balloons, one patterned in wide red and yellow stripes, the other a bright pink with violet zigzags. Pearl looked up at them like a child seeing its first Christmas tree, rapture expressed in her brightening eyes and open mouth that made an 'O' of longing. She turned to Alf who had caught up with her. 'Which one shall we go up in, Alf?'

Alf's mouth opened, too, not with longing but with shock. 'What - me? You won't get me up in one of them things. Nor should you - not at your age.'

'But I told you this morning,' Pearl repeated, annoyed that, as usual, Alf had not been listening.

'That's as maybe, but I never said I'd do it.'

Pearl said no more, charitably putting his mood down to the pains of his arthritis. But a few minutes later, she tried again. 'Do come, Alf,

It'll do you the world of good. You'll see things from quite a different angle.'

Alf shook his head, saying, 'Think I could get up in that contraption - with *my* arthritis?'

Pearl said, 'Well come with me to the rec just to have a look at them.'

Grumbling, he followed her between the colourful stalls, past make-up artists painting fierce animals and Union Jacks on the faces of children, and the band of the Boys' Brigade energetically and patriotically playing 'Rule Britannia'.

Pearl led the way through the gate into the rec; there, the sight of the balloons was even more awesome. Confronted by them in all their girth and glory, even Pearl felt daunted, diminished by their nearness, her easy courage as hollow, now, as the balloons.

Alf looked quite stricken at the sight of the two great creatures, straining to take off; he leaned on his stick and averted his head in final refusal to join her. Pearl knew that, after her earlier determination, she could not back out, nor did she really want to. She felt in her shopping bag and grasped her black, plastic purse. In it was the fare for two people. She had saved it over the past months, secretly, so that it would be a nice surprise for Alf.

She felt guilty at leaving him while she sailed away, up into the blue, but comforted her conscience with the vow that, with Alf's fare saved, she would buy him a new shirt or perhaps one of those posh tweed caps she'd seen in Harper's in town.

'Well then, I'll be off,' she said, firmly.

'You ought to have more sense, going up so high. You'll have one of your turns.'

His warning made Pearl hesitate for a moment with visions of the possible consequences - the anticlimax of a ride, after the flight, to hospital - how would Alf manage without her - their grown-up sons and grandchildren . . . she checked her thoughts. Hadn't Alf, for years, been predicting disasters that never happened?

She clasped her purse to her bosom, feeling that she should make a farewell speech to Alf before her voyage - perhaps even kiss him goodbye. This exciting, dreamed-of flight seemed to demand something to mark its take-off. His look of disapproval, however, stopped her and, instead, she walked purposefully towards the red and yellow balloon whose bright colours seemed to represent her quest for adventure, and paid her fare.

'Come on, love,' one of the men called to her. 'One more for the Skylark - eh?'

Willing hands helped her aboard into the surprisingly capacious basket. There was a frightening roar as the burner was primed and flames shot up into the balloon; then she felt a strange sensation of rising gently without any effort on her part as the balloon, released from the guy ropes, ascended. She peered over the side of the basket and saw, far below, a minute Alf, gazing upwards. She felt something like vertigo - not because of the height they had reached, but because of the expression of anguish on his face.

A rush of guilt assailed her, for her selfishness and her headstrong waywardness that had so often caused rows between her and Alf in the past.

But the exhilaration of flying free, the silent air-voyage, punctuated by the thrust of flame-power, made her forget everything else. Release from the Earth had also released her spirit. Thoughts were replaced by sensations of lightness, of almost reckless delight, a desire to remain aloft forever.

With the other passengers, she looked down at familiar landmarks, made unfamiliar by the different perspective - the town churches and town hall, the High Street and Old Market Place. Pearl could even pick out the small town cottage she and Alf had lived in for the past forty years; impossible, from that height, to realise that it had been home to them and their three, stalwart and growing sons. She felt tears sting her eyes. From up here, all the long struggle that, once commenced, could not be abandoned, the treadmill of scraping a living on Alf's wages, returned to her with its hardships. A great well of emotion surged up inside her and she could no longer see the panorama beneath her through her tears.

'You alright, Gran?' One of the young, male passengers, who looked about the age of her youngest grandson, gave her a look of concern and some alarm.

'Yes, thank you.' Pearl rubbed her eyes with the back of her hand, gave him a half-smile. 'It's just the wind made my eyes sting.'

'Of course.' He put a strong and comforting arm about her shoulders. 'You were brave to come. I wish my gran would. Anyway, we'll soon be back to Earth.'

She gave him a real smile then. 'But I'm - I was enjoying it, really.'

As she spoke, the scene below them seemed, not to become closer, but to expand, bringing back the details; the silence of descent interrupted by short bursts of power to control it. They grounded as softly as they had taken off, with no sense of having arrived. The oak trees looked huge again and everything seemed to crowd closer, giving Pearl a queasy feeling of claustrophobia. The passengers made their descent from their aerial carriage and strolled away, cheerfully, apparently unchanged by the flight away from Earth. But Pearl glanced back at the red and yellow balloon, her home for such a short, heady time, longing to go back and do it all again. She felt in her bag for her purse, still fat with what would have been Alf's fare. He had refused her gift - her hard-saved money for the trip of a lifetime. She half-turned to go back to her red and yellow transport of delight, resentment and the need for another temporary escape overcoming her resolution to buy a present for Alf. The next set of passengers were waiting for a flight in *her* balloon. She took two steps forward, clutching her purse, uncertain what to do.

'Mrs Banks?'

She turned to see a young police officer looking down at her with concern. She could not answer him; the conviction that something terrible had happened to one of her sons - or all of them - and her grandsons - made her dumb with foreboding. She could only nod, imploring him silently to tell her the news that would punish her forever for her past failings.

'Don't look so worried,' the officer said quite cheerfully. 'The First Aid people are helping your husband . . .'

'My husband?' Pearl found it difficult to switch her anxiety to Alf.

'Yes. I'll take you to the First Aid tent.'

'But what happened?'

'I don't rightly know. They asked for you over the loudspeaker, but apparently you weren't back from your trip.'

They edged their way through the crowds whose eyes followed them with interested stares. Pearl, in her stress, felt like a suspected criminal being escorted into custody. There was a small crowd outside the First

Aid tent, alarming her with the thought of what disaster had befallen the grounded Alf while she was airborne. Inside the tent it seemed as if nearly all visitors to the fête had suffered an accident or illness. The small space was crowded with patients, some sitting, some on stretchers. Pearl looked round frantically for Alf. One of the attendants, seeing her with the police officer, approached.

'Mrs Banks? I'm afraid your husband has gone.'

Pearl felt that she was again high up in the balloon, seeing and hearing everything from a great distance.

'Gone? You mean he's - dead?'

'Heavens, no! I'm sorry - I didn't mean to alarm you. As you see, we're inundated. He - Mr Banks fainted and was brought here. We gave him a check-up and there seemed to be nothing to account for it. He insisted on leaving - said something about - um - looking for pearls? I'm afraid I couldn't get him to stay.'

'Pearl,' she corrected. 'My name's Pearl. Oh, dear - where can he be?'

The police officer took charge. 'Probably he's gone back to the rec. I'll go with you - make sure he's found.'

Again, they walked past stalls empty of goods; the crowds were drifting away and the sun had disappeared behind grey clouds.

Pearl, trying to keep up with the officer's long strides, realised belatedly that she had not thought to ask when Alf's fainting fit occurred. How long ago, and had he recovered his senses enough to take the right steps to find her?

They reached the rec. A lone figure was sitting on one of the benches. His back was towards them, but Pearl could feel his dejection. He was looking at the red and yellow balloon that was tethered again, passengers descending from the carriage.

He stood up and began to walk slowly towards the balloon, shading his eyes, obviously trying to see her. Pearl hurried towards him, calling, 'Alf, Alf ! I'm here!'

He turned at the sound of her voice, bewildered by her appearance behind him. He gestured towards the balloon. 'But I remember you going up in it.'

Pearl took his arm and gave it a squeeze. 'So I did, silly. And came down again. The balloon's been up for another trip since.'

She led him back to the bench, smiling her thanks at the police officer, who departed with relief.

'Whatever made you faint like that?'

He wouldn't answer her question, but inwardly, she knew the reason and was touched by his concern for her and ashamed that she had caused him such pain.

Thankfully, they both sat down, like any other elderly couple and let the breeze blow them down memory lane.

CANDYFLOSS CLOUDS
Cliff De Meza

Candyfloss clouds were the only interruption in the bright blue sky. Beneath them was the hustle and bustle of everyday life carrying on regardless. People always found a way of ignoring the bad things that were happening and sometimes the good things as well. The city was buzzing; it was a bank holiday. Practically everybody had the day off work. The children dragged their parents around the shops trying to squeeze extra gifts out of them, and the elderly took time to sit on park benches and let the breeze blow them down memory lane. It was a day when anything could happen and anything was possible.

It was still a little unusual, even in such an enlightened society, for a seventeen-year-old office trainee to have a four-year-old son; who had just started, mornings only, at the local infant school. But then; that was Ellie-May! A very determined girl, she had always thought and acted well ahead of her years, although academically she had never been classed by her teachers as above average. Her quite uncanny perception and her almost clairvoyant powers of prediction, while quite interesting to some, did little to endear her to those nearest and dearest. In fact her mother could get quite frightened, especially when Ellie spoke of serious accidents before they had actually happened. Even when she was only six, Ellie had pulled her mother out of the bus queue saying, 'Don't get on the bus Mummy, it's going to crash into the shop at the bottom of the hill!' It did! Little wonder that Mrs Potter had recurring nightmares, often about being abducted as a teenager.

It was so lovely for mother and son to be enjoying the bank holiday afternoon just walking in the park. They'd fed the ducks, watched people playing bowls and were now enjoying the beauty of the flower beds and the music of the orchestra playing on the bandstand. Little Terry, Terry the Terrible his grandfather called him, had the obligatory ice cream in hand. His mother was holding his other hand as he skipped along at her side.

An elderly woman sitting on a bench looked approvingly at the youthful figures passing: 'See!' said the woman. 'I told you they're not all bad. Just look at that schoolgirl taking her little brother out to play in the park.'

Her husband didn't hear, he was looking up at the sky. 'Just look at those fluffy clouds, all moving quickly from west to east. There must be quite a breeze up there.'

Terry looked up to see what the old gentleman was referring to. He pointed skywards. 'Daddy!' he said excitedly.

As Ellie-May looked up, one cloud stopped moving briefly, then it started to descend towards the park. It enveloped the large, main lawn beyond the trees with a cold, freezing mist, and all the people playing ball games or picnicking there moved towards the bandstand area, where the sun was still shining brightly.

'Come on then!' Ellie started running through the trees and into the cloud, almost dragging little Terry behind her, but he was just as eager to go there, and was running as fast as his little legs would carry him. They ran up a shiny, metal ramp and into a large hallway lit by a strange, bluish light. There was a whirring sound and the ramp folded up forming a closed door behind them.

Suddenly a voice seemed to come from all around them. 'Hello Terry! Are you coming up to see Daddy then?'

'Yes!' Terry jumped in the air with excitement and ran to push a large, red square on the far wall.

'Bring Mummy up with you then, there's someone here I want her to meet.'

A door slid open and they stepped into an elevator. It moved sideways, then ascended, then moved forwards. It stopped and the door opened. They were in a large, octagonal room, which seemed to be a cross between the bridge of a ship and the flight deck of a large aircraft. All very high tech, with push buttons, stubby little levers and visual displays everywhere. There were two pilots' seats at the main driving console, behind that, slightly elevated, on a platform was the Commander's seat and console, and there were four other seats each at a console for a specialist officer, navigator, engineer, communications officer and the defensive systems co-ordinator. In the central area behind the Commander's platform was a lounge area, equipped for rest and relaxation. Four six-seater settees covered in a bright, yellow material formed a square. There sat Daddy in his pink catsuit uniform of a Commander in the Zerkon Intergalactic Fleet. Next to him sat a sweet, little teenaged girl wearing the uniform of a local comprehensive school in the city. The other six officers on duty on the bridge were busy doing their pre-flight checks for their return voyage home, while their twenty off-duty colleagues were either sleeping in their quarters, having meals, working out in the gym or just relaxing, each according to their duty watch.

Daddy rose to his feet as Terry ran to him. 'Terry, you little rascal! How you've grown in the last three months since I saw you on Zerkon at Christmas.'

'He goes to school part-time now, but he's started to levitate and transport. The teacher says she thinks he's just hyperactive.' Ellie-May sounded concerned.

'Oh, he'll grow out of that very quickly. They always do. It's just the first excitement of starting school.' He turned to Terry. 'You must watch what the other kids do, and do the same as them. Nothing more. D'you understand Terry my lad! Do nothing that the other kids don't do, then they won't suspect that you are any different to them.'

'Yes Daddy. I'll try and remember. Can we go out and play ball in the park now please?'

'Certainly my son! I could do with a good kick about after the long voyage. We can leave Mummy to talk to this nice lady. Come on then!' They both disappeared into the elevator.

Ellie-May looked at the girl and smiled. 'So, you've been to Zerkon then! What's your name dear?'

'Oh! It was so beautiful. All those lovely buildings made of shiny titanium, and the beautiful plants and flowers. Such loving people too. I stayed with a nice family who had a big dwelling unit in the country, near the giant cabbage forest. They had their own transitpod, and they took me all over the place. I saw the Mammoths, the Dodo birds and the Crockofish in the wildlife reserve. They took me to the Yellow Lakes and the Bamboo Mountains. Another time we went into Zertina City, to the Earth Sciences Research Institute.' She thought for a moment, her gaze almost transfixed. 'Most of all I enjoyed playing with their children, little boy and girl twins of about seven. Their pet lizard named Donko always slept on my bed. They were very difficult to play hide-and-seek with though, they would keep disappearing, transporting through walls and sometimes I would find them floating above me just looking down and laughing.' Her face was a picture of delight from the fond memories. She smiled at Ellie. 'By the way, I'm Sarah, and I'm in the sixth form at City Road Comp.' She looked down at her uniform. 'My mum will kill me! I've been away for six weeks - I think!'

'No! It's OK. Please don't worry Sarah, let me explain. When you step off this craft, it will be exactly the same date and time as when you boarded it. In your case you will not remember a thing and you will never return to Zerkon. You may get the odd, funny dreams, I know my mother did, but otherwise you will return to your usual life on Earth. When you're older and in a stable relationship, your first child will be a girl, and she will be a first generation Earth-Zerkonite like me. They will have programmed that into you at the research institute. Like me, your daughter will have extra-sensory perception and be able to predict the future, and she will have a baby boy in her very early teens who will be a second generation Earth-Zerkonite, like my son Terry. She will know who the Zerkonite father is, and must have the baby before she is fifteen, or the powers will not transfer from father to son. Her son will have extraordinary powers, like the people you've met on Zerkon, but he'll have to keep them hidden on Earth until "Peace on Earth Day", when all will be revealed.'

'Do you go to Zerkon sometimes yourself, or is it just the little boy who goes?'

'Well Sarah, obviously I went there when I was twelve to meet with Terry's father to be, Tyno the commander of this ship. He was only a senior pilot then. I've been back once since, to stay with Tyno's Zerkonite wife and his other three children. Terry, on the other hand, has been there twice more without me. He loves it there, but his job is to be here on Earth.'

'Sarah! Ellie! Come and look at this girls.' The communications officer called them to her console. The large video screen in front of them showed the activities in the park. There were Tyno and Terry kicking a ball about, while half the off-duty Zerkonite crew were sitting in deck chairs listening to the band. All in their distinctive colourful catsuit uniforms. 'The people just think that they're in fancy dress, and waiting to take part in the bank holiday parade. It's astonishing!' She turned to the girls and laughed. 'I've sent a subliminal thought transference to them, telling them it's time they came aboard and reminding them to come on foot and not to transport.'

They all returned to the craft as instructed, and all the fond farewells were said. Terry didn't really want to leave.

'Can I come and stay with you again soon? Please Daddy!'

'We'll see! Next year perhaps! If you've been a good boy at school that is!'

Ellie-May, Terry and Sarah walked out of the freezing cloud and into the sunlit park. The cloud lifted and joined its squadron in the clear blue sky.

The old gentleman looked up. 'Oh look! The wind must have changed. Those fluffy clouds are moving east to west now and going faster than ever.'

His wife looked at the three youngsters. 'Those nice children have got their sister with them now dear. I wonder why she's in school uniform on a bank holiday?'

At last the old man was listening. 'Perhaps her school choir is in the parade, dear.'

'Excuse me dear!' The old lady beckoned to Sarah who came over. 'Is your school choir singing here today?'

'No, I don't think so! Sorry!' Sarah smiled. She liked old people, she found them interesting.

'Well, I mustn't keep you dear, you must catch up with your brother and sister before you lose sight of them.'

Sarah looked towards Ellie-May and Terry. 'Oh! I'm not with them. I don't know them. They could be from another planet for all I know!'

After all said and done! It was just another bank holiday in the park, with the orchestra playing and candyfloss clouds floating across the clear blue sky.

POOR VAN GOGH!
S V Batten

Candyfloss clouds were the only interruption in the bright blue sky. Beneath them was the hustle and bustle of everyday life carrying on regardless. People always found a way of ignoring the bad things that were happening and sometimes the good things as well. The city was buzzing; it was a bank holiday. Practically everybody had the day off work. The children dragged their parents around the shops trying to squeeze extra gifts out of them, and the elderly took time to sit on park benches and let the breeze blow them down memory lane. It was a day when anything could happen and anything was possible.

I was waiting for Sara at the Westmoreland Park entrance. She was late, which circumstance had given me a minute or two of inactivity in which my mind had wandered. The brilliant sunshine - so rare on a northeast England bank holiday - made every colour glow, every texture scintillate and every shape vibrate. Each glance - whether straight ahead or to left or right - revealed, it seemed, a new oil painting by Van Gogh, where shape or form, texture or surface and hue or colour rejoiced in a vibrant vitality. I knew most of his famous works of art by heart. I was no expert - as I'd mocked myself often in private saying so - but I knew very well what I liked and couldn't resist! That poor, lonely, misunderstood Dutchman had often led me to realise that he'd never seen the world about him in the same way that anyone else had. He'd tried to tell what he saw - but nobody had listened - until too late!

When I'd arranged to meet Sara, it had been to try and patch up our recent differences. From the time we met - two years ago on a blind date engineered by my sister Melissa and her boyfriend Fraser - we'd made a good match of it without having to strive too hard to reach an understanding.

Sometimes, it seemed as though there was a stable bond between us - as well as physical awareness that was mutual, we had common interests in musical preferences, travel plans and ideas of how to make the world a better place. But, sometimes - especially in the last few weeks - we were divided and almost coldly hostile over future plans, frequency of dates or meetings and what to talk about. I suppose neither of us had completely, irrevocably decided that our lives would never be divergent. The magic of that first meeting, the bliss of that idyllic rapport and the comfort of that mutual support, affection and first love did not appear to be likely to be replaced by commitment and undying dependency.

To add to this - or should I say to complicate this - there was Teresa.

The park was nearly as full of activity as the City Centre. The neatly bordered grassy areas beneath the picturesque groups of trees were animatedly peopled as young and old bathed in sunshine - more than one or two young men and your women seeking a ninety-nine percent all-over tan were occupying secluded places. I caught another glimpse or two of how Van Gogh might have seen it all, especially in about 1888 when he moved to Arles and he was thirty-five-years old, having decided to devote his life to painting some seven years earlier. The colours were more than vibrant - they were almost luminous, as I glanced around. I caught myself thinking that they should be captured in some way so that the throbbing vitality to the Westmoreland Park could be encapsulated - and stolen from the passage of time - forever.

'Hello, Marc.'

Teresa, standing in front of me, startled me. She - of the black hair, creamy complexion, red lips and dark, unfathomable, provocative eyes - became an essential ingredient of the glowing, sun-kissed panorama.

'Oh, hello Teresa! You made me jump. I was miles away!'

'I came into town to catch the exhibition at the City Hall. It being a bank holiday, I took the day off!'

Teresa ran her beautician salon in Fask Street. By all accounts, her clientele enjoyed excellent beauty treatment there.

'That's the Impressionist exhibition, isn't it?'

'Yes - but they've included "classical" paintings of the same period. It's a touring exhibition sponsored by the Royal Academy.'

'I'd like to see that.'

'You said you liked paintings.'

'A hidden penchant.'

'Being a "merchant adventurer" at work doesn't mean you can't admire artists and their work in your spare time.'

'You remembered!'

'What?'

'That I said I was a "merchant adventurer"!'

'You work in an import/export company.'

'Yes, but I only said I was a "merchant adventurer" in order to impress you.'

'And you did!'

We laughed together. That was something Sara and I rarely did - or ever had - I wanted to say. And yet - had I ever tried to show Sara that playful, wilful streak in my mind that made me swap reality for fantasy or romance in extravagant words about a secret longing? Perhaps that same streak made me see a possible Van Gogh treatment for a scene Van Gogh could never have seen.

'Why don't you come to the exhibition with me?'

'I said I'd meet Sara.'

'But she's late, isn't she?'

'Yes.'

'Perhaps she's not going to turn up.'

'Oh, I expect something's detained her.'

Teresa's dress was patterned with large, soft, pink roses on a black background and the material shimmered in the golden sunshine. It emphasised her lissom figure and each subtle contour as she stood swaying ever so slightly in high-heeled pink sandals. She looked like the models in the TV advertisements - and like a Titian nymph or goddess at the same time. Unsought, this moment seemed to be a destined meeting which would change my feelings forever.

I was not immune to allurement. Nor had been Van Gogh. After he had finished his schooling at the age of fifteen - a solitary boy capped by close-cropped, red hair, with deep-set eyes and a stooping walk - he had worked at Gupil's art dealers in The Hague until he was nineteen for four years. At the age of nineteen, in 1872, he had moved to Gupil's art dealers in London. There he had fallen in love with Ursula Loyer - and she had not returned his love. The solitary-minded young man had been rendered even more hopeless. My perception of the animation of the scene around me and Teresa was not affected by my recollection of the greyness of that episode in that lonely young man's life.

'Are you sure you won't come with me to the exhibition, Marc?'

Teresa's voice sounded as if she was offering all kinds of inducement to cement a new attraction and a future understanding.

In 1880, after Van Gogh had finally decided to become an artist, he had been rejected after proposing marriage to a widowed cousin - that is, he had been spurned a second time as a prospective lover and protector. These rejections were biographical facts. But there must have been more moments with other women or girls when he saw with pleasure - as a man - and as an artist - even if it was only for a moment - just as I was now looking at Teresa.

I replied, 'No,' to Teresa's invitation. So she left me and started to walk away. I wasn't sure whether I was pleased or sorry to see her go. And I am still not sure why I had said no.

My brother Tom, at twenty-five was two years younger than I. He had been married to Julie for nearly two years now. My sister, Beth, at twenty-three was four years younger than I and she had been married to Robert for about a year now. I'd listened to what they had told me before and after each of them had been married. Had they each passed through a phase similar to that in which Sara and I seemed to be trapped? And had there been a 'Teresa' for Tom, or a 'Terry' for Beth?

'Hello, Marc,' said Sara. 'I'm sorry I'm late. The shop was so crowded - probably because the sale started today. And it's such a nice day - the sun's really warm - everyone is having a good time. I know it isn't your birthday yet - it's another three weeks isn't it! But I knew what I wanted to get you - so I've got it! Here it is!'

Sara put a flat, oblong parcel wrapped in a cheerful, colourful paper into my not-quite-ready hands. It felt fairly heavy and solidly compact.

'They offered to wrap it for me - so I said yes!' There is something else, but I didn't want to carry it now - so I said you would collect it yourself later today. They're very nice in there - an old man and his niece, someone said - but it was so crowded you couldn't really talk to them.'

'Sara! Slow down! Thanks for the present! But we were supposed to be going to have a serious talk.'

'What is there to talk about?'

'We seem to have been having problems.'

'We suit each other, you and I. I knew from the beginning we were going to get on well together! Just lately, it's slowed down a bit, but that's because we haven't been sure of the future! We'll get married at Christmas - I always fancied a white velvet dress - and we'll be settled and happy after that! So there's nothing to discuss!'

I felt as I had done before when Sara and her blue eyes were sparkling and her voice was like singing and her blonde hair was swinging as her whole being was almost dancing. How could anything ever lose its sparkle if Sara was with me?

'So there's nothing to discuss?' I asked, though I knew already what she would reply.

'No!' Sara replied emphatically. 'So open your present!'

'What is it?' I asked slowly as I began to remove the wrapping paper, but Sara wouldn't answer me, though her expression was a rare mixture of merriment, love, pleasure, excitement and trust.

I looked at the japanned, flat box and was filled with conjecture and rising excitement and hot anticipation. I opened the box slowly.

'That's right! It's a paintbox! A starter's oil painting kit - a palette and brushes - and ten tubes of paint! The old man in the shop said it was excellent value - and I got it cheap because of the sale! There's some blank canvasses for you to pick up later!'

'But - but - how did you know I wanted to paint?'

'I've seen you looking at paintings - and views! So now you can paint your own!'

'Oh, Sara, *thank you*!' I said as I hugged her - and the paintbox.

Poor Van Gogh! If only he'd had a 'Sara'!

But afterwards, I thought that I'd wanted to think of Van Gogh as a perpetually-tormented soul, unlucky enough never to fall in love and have his love returned - I'd wanted him not to be like me, even though, somehow, I'd got it into my head that I would be able to paint pictures like his.

Maybe I should not judge him. Maybe I should simply accept what he had revealed as his vision of the things and people contemporary with him during his lifetime and understand it as an expression of a statement of one man's search for truth.

Poor Van Gogh! How swift was I to dismiss him as tormented when all he had tried to do was to record what he had seen - and be himself!

ROBERT PRUETT'S NEW CAR
Garry Knowles

Candyfloss clouds were the only interruption in the bright blue sky. Beneath them was the hustle and bustle of everyday life carrying on regardless. People always found a way of ignoring the bad things that were happening and sometimes the good things as well. The city was buzzing; it was a bank holiday. Practically everybody had the day off work. The children dragged their parents around the shops trying to squeeze extra gifts out of them, and the elderly took time to sit on park benches and let the breeze blow them down memory lane. It was a day when anything could happen and anything was possible.

Not the individual in question, but another one, Robert Pruett, stood at his front door admiring the new, shiny red Nissan Primera Gti saloon.

It had just been delivered ten minutes earlier and was now sitting on his drive. The last time he'd owned a Japanese car was almost ten years ago, a tatty yellow Datsun Cherry with more rust than metal. That was the main reason he'd scrapped the lemon-coloured heap (the rust that is). Well, it wasn't so much he'd scrapped it, it was more a case of it scrapped itself. He realised it wasn't going to see another day's motoring when he clipped the kerb outside Woolworth's and the front, near-side wing fell off. Closely followed by the boot, the bonnet, the rear window, the back fender and both rear wheels. After that he'd consoled himself with two Fords, three Hillmans, a Skoda, a Landrover and a VW Beetle. Oh and a little, funny-shaped thing from Russia. He vowed and declared never to buy another Datsun car, and to be quite honest he didn't realise till he paid the final instalment on his new Primera, that 'Nissan' was actually the same motor manufacturer that was once upon a time the dreaded 'Datsun' company.

When fear showed in his face the salesman picked up on his anxiety straight away. 'Don't worry Mr Pruett,' he reassured. 'Nissan now build probably the finest cars in the world. That's why they changed their name, they didn't want their mistakes of the 70s influencing their sales of the 21st century, so they changed their name from Datsun to Nissan.'

As Robert looked admiringly at his gleaming new car he had to admit this was a fine-looking car. The sun was shining, he'd the whole weekend off, and how he was going to enjoy driving through the countryside showing off his new purchase.

As he climbed into his shiny new chariot, the smell of fine calfskin leather encapsulated his nostrils, the dashboard encased him in technology and he felt like the fifth and ultimate captain of the Starship Enterprise - Beam me up Scottie!

Placing the key in the ignition he heard the temperature control module whirr into the air conditioning mode, he smiled.

But as he turned the ignition key the final click to set the 1600 thoroughbreds into motion, his ears were not met by the expected cacophony of Japanese craftsmanship. Just a loud bang followed by a cloud of black smoke and the sound of someone throwing three handfuls of loose change into a steel dustbin.

Sitting in a state of shock he watched the candyfloss clouds turn a muddy brown and the blue sky turn grey. This surely was a day when almost anything could happen, and he was sure it had.

Robert walked the three miles to the Nissan garage, which if nothing else, gave his raging temper time to calm down slightly. After all, as far as he was concerned, the worse thing that could happen, had.

'What do you mean, you don't stock parts for the Primera,' Robert screamed at the spotty-faced fool in blue overalls, (grinning from the opposite side of the counter) and wearing a 'Derek' name tag.

As Robert lunged at spotty Derek's throat the manager appeared.

'Come, come Mr Pruett, what seems to be the problem?'

After Robert had explained that his £21,000 pride and joy had committed suicide on his drive, and without even turning a wheel. The manager agreed to 'Drag it in and have a tinker about' (which made Robert's eyes water at the thought).

That night though Robert didn't sleep a wink, instead he stood looking at the empty space where once stood his pride and joy, and was reduced almost to tears.

The next morning he was waiting by the showroom entrance as the Nissan staff started work. 'What's happening about my car?' he shouted to the manager as he parked his car.

'Don't worry Mr Pruett,' the manager said. 'No doubt the wheels are in motion as we speak. Come through to the showroom and have a coffee while I check on the progress.'

Robert knew it was bad news by the look on the manager's face as he reappeared.

'A slight problem I'm afraid Mr Pruett,' he said smiling. 'The parts we needed for your gearbox are still in Japan.'

Robert was speechless.

The manager sat adjacent to Robert as he explained the situation. 'The storeman has contacted our head office in Japan, as we speak, the parts are being loaded onto a private jet.' Looking at his watch he smiled and continued with his feeble explanation. 'If all goes well, the parts will be here later today, so you'll be able to drive your car away tomorrow morning.'

Robert was absolutely seething by now. 'It'd better be,' he said, rising to his feet, 'or there'll be hell to pay.' And with that he stormed from the showroom.

Nagoya Shikoku was the second-in-command aboard the private jet, which flew regularly from Tokyo to London. Their flight had been delayed slightly while they waited for an urgent box of automotive parts. Once the box had been loaded and they were cleared for take-off, Nagoya went to the rear of the aeroplane to fetch his captain (Kyoto Osumi), a glass of iced tea. It was at this point he thought he heard a clicking sound, then assuming he had imagined it he went about his chores.

Ten hours later as the plane passed over the South coast of England, the clicking started again and an orange light began to flash on the control panel of the private jet. Nagoya reached for the flight manual and began searching for the fault-finding sheet. Within a matter of seconds the orange light turned to red, an audible screeching began to sound in the cockpit, and the clicking turned to banging.

'Forget that,' shouted the Captain (and pointed to several dials on the control panel, which had now begun to turn themselves off). 'We've lost an engine, and with the weight we're carrying we'll never make it to London.'

The young co-pilot felt his limbs begin to shake as the jet began to descend. 'What shall I do?' he screamed to the more experienced Captain. 'Are we going to die?'

The Captain turned to face him. 'We are if you don't calm down and start throwing some of the cargo out of the rear door.'

Nagoya ran to the rear of the aircraft and began to jettison some of their precious cargo.

Bartholomew Todd was enjoying the rare British sun as he cycled down the winding road from Longmoor to Liphook in Hampshire. The last few years had been relatively unkind to him in many ways. The start of his bad luck was almost three years ago to the day; he'd thrown a ball for his pet spaniel, 'Lucky' not realising that 20 yards from him was a landmine left over from recent military manoeuvres. As the ball hit the ground, Lucky hit the mine.

The bomb disposal expert who attended the scene said 'I'll be cleaning bits of blooming dog up for the next three weeks.'

Then there was an incident with his car 13 months later. He told the fire chief he could have sworn he'd applied the handbrake. His car had rolled down the drive hitting the side of his house; it had exploded into a ball of flames, and completely destroyed not only his house but also his neighbours' on each side as well.

Then last year when at last he thought his luck had changed for the better, disaster struck again.

A beautiful lady young lady had started working in his bank, as far as Bartholomew was concerned she was the Mrs Right he'd spent his whole life looking for. After a whirlwind romance they were married two weeks later.

However, fate was ready to deal him the losing hand again, but this time on his wedding night. As he lay in the bridal suite with his new bride, he realised something was not quite right, but after confronting the love of his life with his quandary, he was appalled by her reply.

Jane confessed that once upon a time she used to be Jonathan.

But no amount of make-up could hide her 12 o'clock shadow and hairy legs, (and many other unspeakable bits) and the last she saw of Bartholomew was him running screaming into the night. But now as he cycled along enjoying the freedom of the open road, he was able to smile at his past misfortunes. Well, that was until the box of Japanese gearbox parts that Nagoya had just thrown from 18,000 feet hit him squarely on the head.

Robert was also enjoying the beautiful summer's afternoon strolling down the country lanes of Hampshire; the only thought in his head was of numerous mechanics working frantically on his Primera. His thoughts were instantly shattered as he walked round a bend in the road to be confronted by police cars and ambulances. As Robert walked closer he noticed parts of high-tech Japanese machinery lying over the road. Paramedics and doctors were working desperately on the battered body of the previously happy cycling Bartholomew.

A policeman stepped from a car and prevented Robert from proceeding any further. 'I'm sorry, Sir, you can't go any further, he said (holding his arm across Robert's chest).

Robert looked at the mangled body of the bank manager on the floor. 'What on Earth has happened?' he asked the young constable.

The policeman removed his helmet and looked in the direction of the candyfloss clouds, 'Beats me, Sir, but by all accounts it seems to have been raining Datsun cogs.'

IT CAME FROM OUTER SPACE
Melanie M Burgess

Candyfloss clouds were the only interruption in the bright blue sky. Beneath them was the hustle and bustle of everyday life carrying on regardless. People always found a way of ignoring the bad things that were happening and sometimes the good things as well. The city was buzzing; it was a bank holiday. Practically everybody had the day off work. The children dragged their parents around the shops trying to squeeze extra gifts out of them, and the elderly took time to sit on park benches and let the breeze blow them down memory lane. It was a day when anything could happen and anything was possible.

And as often happens in fiction but rarely in real life, a spaceship appeared over the city.

Everyone stopped what they were doing to stare in wonder at the large ship. Slowly it lowered a long staircase and two men descended.

They did not need to ask to be taken to the leader. He was away for the summer break in any case, as was half the Cabinet. A leader of sorts did appear in the form of the local mayor.

'Do not worry. We come in peace.' They had intercepted a lot of old movies over the years. 'We have been monitoring your planet for some time now and feel that we can offer help. Our technology is much more advanced than yours.'

The first alien, who actually looked human, said, 'We have taken on your appearance so that you will not be alarmed. I have taken the name of Bob and this is Fred.'

'We'll have to get the Prime Minister back of course,' The Mayor spluttered. 'But in the meantime, welcome to our world. If you give me a few hours, no doubt we can get a civic reception organised.'

'We do not come looking for honours. We only come to share. You have much poverty. Much crime and many wars. You are choking your planet with fumes. All this we have eliminated from our world.'

'Now listen a minute, Mate,' John, the union leader, stepped forward. 'We have a great country here. We don't need people coming down telling us what to do.' There was a nodding of heads. People were in agreement. 'It's one thing to grumble about your own country but quite another for strangers to do so and aliens at that.'

The aliens seemed to catch the drift of the mood and Bob said 'Pardon us. We do not mean to offend. We only come to help.'

'We'll have to get the government back. We can't make those sorts of decisions,' the Mayor muttered.

So it was decided that Bob and Fred could have a tour of the city whilst the Cabinet and Prime Minister were urged to return from holiday.

The American President arrived in the meantime, as did a delegation from China, India, Pakistan, Russia, Africa and Europe.

The city was soon crawling with diplomats. 'What weapons of war do you have?' asked the diplomats.

'Powerful weapons which we no longer use. We were destroying the universe before we came to our senses.'

'Could we have some of those?'

'We no longer need weapons. We are at harmony with ourselves and others. We no longer have arguments on our planet, we have eliminated greed, power, all the things that caused us to argue and fight.'

'Have you got new toys?' the children asked. 'Can we see what you have? Are they bigger than our toys? Are they better?'

'We entertain ourselves with music and the arts. We visit each other and have long and philosophical conversations. Even our young people. We have no need for your television, cars or skateboards. They caused disharmony amongst our young.'

'What a boring place your world must be,' the children opined.

'On the contrary, we are at peace and are all in perfect harmony.'

'What did you use to control your children?' the parents asked.

'We are not allowed to hit them anymore and they do as they please.'

'Have you something to discipline the children with?'

'We do not need to discipline the young. They have been brought up with love from an early age. They respond to that. They would not think of disobeying us and making us sad.'

The parents looked doubtful. Perhaps the aliens did not know the concept of teenagers.

'Can you bring us long life and our youth back?' asked the old people. 'We want to be young and healthy again.'

'Youth is not the answer. What about the wisdom you have acquired with age?'

'Most of us have only acquired wrinkles,' said the spokesperson for the elderly.

'But there is beauty in that as well. We do not repress old age on our planet. Without old age we would not have people who know our history.'

The elderly muttered. It sounded like a load of nonsense to them.

'Space technology,' piped up one of the diplomats. 'Give us your space technology so that we can go and conquer other worlds.'

'We use our spaceship to spread peace and harmony, not to conquer.'

'Well, we'll use it for that then. Tell us how to make our spaceships better.'

'I do not think you will use that technology wisely just yet,' Bob answered.

'Coming down here. Telling us what's good for us and what's not.' The people were grumbling again.

Fred was trying to control the children who were swarming over the ship. 'Please children, be careful what you are touching. Some of the equipment is very sensitive. Do you not listen to your elders?'

Obviously not. The children continued to poke about and look in cupboards.

The diplomats had been arguing amongst themselves. Now they said, 'If you can't give us space technology, or weapons of war, or disciplinary methods for our children or new toys or youth, what can you give us?'

Here Bob was on solid ground, so he thought. 'We can give you the technology to build machines that will bring water to your deserts. Or create good in barren regions.'

'We have food and water,' the people said.

'Not all of your people. There are millions starving. We have monitored your planet. There are great regions of desert or barren land that are crying out to be cultivated.'

'We suppose so,' the people said reluctantly.

'Also we can tell you how we stopped warring.'

The diplomats looked horrified. 'Without war how do we get rid of the surplus population,' they asked. 'How do we make money without the arms trade?'

'We will show you other enterprises. Other means of making money. Or how to get rid of money altogether. How to live in harmony. Each person having the same. No more need for greed or war.'

The diplomats consulted amongst themselves. Eventually they even thought to consult the people.

'Can you, er, leave a calling card or something?'

Bob looked amazed. 'We can give you a means of recalling us, yes. But why don't you let us do things now, whilst we are here?'

'We'll have to take it under advisement. We don't want to rush into anything. A big decision and all that.'

Reluctantly, Bob agreed. He gave their scientists the co-ordinates for recalling them. This, the scientists promptly lost. Fortunately Bob did not see that.

Then he and Fred evicted the children from the spaceship, said their goodbyes to the people who had mostly all dispersed by now anyway, and left Earth.

'I cannot understand why they did not want our help,' Bob said. 'Look at what those children have done to the ship. It will take me weeks to repair it.'

'I will help you.'

'No you will not. You have done enough already. I told you to go to Mars but oh no, you insisted on Earth.'

'Oh, that is right. Blame me now.'

'Well at least on Mars we would have been dealing with microbes. Microbes are always grateful.

BANK HOLIDAY MONDAY, 2002
Jenny Porteous

Candyfloss clouds were the only interruption in the bright blue sky.
Beneath them was the hustle and bustle of everyday life carrying on
regardless. People always found a way of ignoring the bad things that
were happening and sometimes the good things as well. The city was
buzzing; it was a bank holiday. Practically everybody had the day off
work. The children dragged their parents around the shops trying to
squeeze extra gifts out of them, and the elderly took time to sit on park
benches and let the breeze blow them down memory lane. It was a day
when anything could happen and anything was possible.

August Bank Holiday 2002, a glorious day, warm and sunny after a
wet dismal start to the month. Busy shoppers thronged the streets,
happy to be out on such a day. Children laughed and chattered.
Everyone was in holiday mood. It was a day for families, but I was
alone. I couldn't remember the last holiday I had spent alone, it had
always been me and Steve, or me, Steve and the boys, happy times of
fun and laughter, gone forever now. I wandered aimlessly through the
busy street, feeling depressed and sorry for myself, trying to decide
what to buy for my lonely dinner that evening. Shopping for one was
not a task I enjoyed, and right now I felt I never wanted to eat again.
The twins were spending the holiday weekend with their father, he had
promised to take them to the local theme park to celebrate their recent
twelfth birthday and, although I missed them terribly, I was glad to get a
break from their constant questions. Why had Daddy gone away?
Where had he gone? When was he coming back? How could I tell them
the father they adored was never coming back, how could I tell them he
had chosen to start a new life with another woman half my age, and
only six years older than themselves? I had lived in a daze for the past
three weeks, ever since that awful day when Steve had come home in
the middle of the afternoon to pack his bags and tell me he was leaving.
There had been no warning, no tell-tale signs of what had been going on
right under my nose. Although, if I had stopped to think about it, I
should have been suspicious of the amount of overtime he had suddenly
had to do. For almost six months he had been staying later and later at
the office, but he always had an explanation, and, he assured me, he
would make it up to me and the twins, the extra money would buy a lot

of the little luxuries we could not afford before. But there never were any 'little luxuries' and the extra money did not materialise either, no wonder, he was probably spending it all on his new love.

On a sudden impulse, I decided to abandon my shopping and walk down to the park on the outskirts of town where we had spent so many happy hours. Steve and I had met in that park, I was taking a lunch break and he was walking his dog, we got chatting and from there on it was a typical storybook romance. We started dating, fell in love, got married and our joy was complete with the birth of our twins. Now the joy had gone out of my life forever. How could I be happy without the man I loved more than anyone else? Yes, I had the twins to love and care for but that was not quite the same, even they could not fill the lonely empty space in my heart.

Manor Park was one of my favourite places. Our special place, a green haven filled with peace and tranquillity, but not today, for me it seemed to have lost some of its beauty. Something was different, something was wrong. The trees were the same, the grass was as green as ever, ducks were still swimming on the little lake with the mermaid fountain and people still walked and talked and enjoyed the tranquillity. But not me, I had never felt so lost and alone in my entire life. I wandered around for a while, and then sat down on a bench by the lake to watch the ducks floating on the cool water as I recalled the happy memories of yesterday.

'Buy a spray of white heather from an old lady, my dear?'

The voice at my side brought me out of my reverie with a start and I turned my gaze towards the speaker. She was dressed entirely in black, her flowing dress reached just below the tops of her old-fashioned button-up boots, a short linen cloak draped her skinny shoulders, and straggly wisps of snowy-white hair peeped beneath her large bonnet. Her brown Romany skin was wrinkled and weather-beaten, her frail body bent almost double. She looked like she could have been around for a million years. But it was her eyes that held my attention, dark ebony eyes peering at me from that wizened old face with a large beak-like nose. Mesmerised by this strange woman, I reached for my empty shopping bag and took a coin from my purse which I exchanged for something that vaguely resembled a spray of white heather, although it looked almost as faded and worn as the bearer. The old witch smiled as she tucked the coin in her pocket and her bony hand reached out to touch mine. 'Bad things have happened, but good things are coming, you will see my dear, you will see.' The beady eyes took on a soft glow as she gazed at me for a moment and then she was gone. Just gone, she had vanished before my very eyes as though she had never been there.

As I stared at the tatty white heather in my hand I suddenly felt very strange, the trees around the lake began to sway, although there wasn't even a slight breeze to disturb them, the air around me became hushed and eerily still, everything became still, so still, as I felt myself drifting away. Falling, falling back through time and space, right back to that day almost twenty years ago when I had sat at this very spot to watch the ducks, while I took a break from the office desk to eat my lunch. The lake was the same, except there was no mermaid fountain, the ducks, the trees, people walking in the sunshine and me, a young sixteen-year-old who had just left school, and started her first job. How grown up I felt then, the world was my oyster as they say, and I was going to go far. I knew exactly what would happen next. I had been there before, so it was no surprise when a small black and white dog bounded up and dropped a ball at my feet, wagging his tail and barking excitedly, eagerly waiting for a game.

'I'm so sorry, I hope Benji isn't being a nuisance?' The tall dark-haired young man picked up the ball and tossed it in the direction of the lake as he spoke; Benji scampered after it, still wagging his tail and barking madly.

And so I sat there, as though in a trance, watching the familiar scenes pass before me. The story of my life unfolded like a moving picture book. The young man became my husband, the twins came into the picture, two beautiful boys. I watched them growing from babies to toddlers, the first day at school, the happy times and a few sad times when one or other was ill, or a favourite pet died. Birthday parties, Christmas trees and presents, joyful family scenes that made me smile. Then, all too soon, came the tears as the unfolding story reached that awful afternoon only three weeks ago.

Like an action replay on a sports programme I watched as Steve packed a few belongings into a bag, telling me he would come back for the rest of his stuff. Then he was gone and I stood alone, tears streaming down my face. At that moment the picture show stopped.

A hand touched my shoulder and I turned to see the old woman in black standing by my side. 'Good things are coming my dear, watch and see.' Her weather-beaten face broke into a smile as she gently clasped my hand. 'Watch and see,' she said again as the trees around the lake began to sway, and I felt myself drifting away. I closed my eyes, I was moving forward, onwards, through uncharted time and space. The bench that I sat on was old and rickety now, the mermaid fountain no longer sprayed glistening water into the air, like the seat, it was definitely the worse for wear, but the ducks still swam, dipping and diving in the Bank Holiday sunshine.

The twins had grown now; at twenty-two Steve Junior was the image of his father, tall and dark-haired with that familiar smile I loved so much. Richard, with his lighter brown hair was more like me. I watched as they spread the picnic lunch on the blanket on the ground, chatting and laughing with the two pretty girls that accompanied them. I turned to smile contentedly at the handsome blond-haired man by my side. He slipped his arm around my shoulder as we sat in silence each preoccupied with our thoughts, yet cocooned in a web of happiness. Happiness I thought I would never find again. I thought I could never be happy without Steve. A small girl with long blonde curls and blue eyes rushed up to us, a black and white puppy bounding playfully at her feet. As my companion reached out to pat the dog's head I saw the tattoo on the back of his right hand, a Celtic cross. Then the trees around the lake began to sway, the image faded before my eyes and I was back in the park on Bank Holiday Monday 2002.

The ducks were swimming idly on the cool water of the lake, the mermaid fountain sent sprays of water into the warm air, people walked in the sunshine, children played happily on the swings. Just an ordinary bank holiday. No old lady with white heather, no blond-haired stranger at my side. I tried to put the weird experience out of my mind, telling myself I must have fallen asleep. It was all a dream, and I still had the shopping to do. I had to eat for the twins' sake, we needed each other.

Perhaps it was the heat, my unhappy state of mind, or a combination of both, but suddenly I felt light-headed and faint. I could not get that strange living dream out of my mind. A cup of coffee was what I needed, and a sandwich, I hadn't eaten since the previous night. There was a little tea shop by the park gate, Steve and I had been there so many times. I had not been near the place since he left. Was it really just three weeks ago? It felt more like three years. Automatically, it seemed, my footsteps took me back. I did not recognise the man behind the counter, tall with fair hair and gorgeous blue eyes that lit up when he smiled. I sat down at the table by the window, lost in my thoughts as I waited for my order. I was jerked out of my daydreaming and my heart almost stopped beating when he placed the plate in front of me. 'Enjoy your lunch,' he said, smiling broadly.

'I will,' I replied, staring in amazement at his hand. His right hand, on the back of which was the tattoo I had seen just a few minutes earlier. A Celtic cross!

I finished my shopping in a daze. What had happened to me as I sat on the bench in the park? Surely I had simply fallen asleep in the sun and that strange experience was nothing more than a dream? The fair-haired waiter with the unusual tattoo was purely a coincidence. Time travel was a thing that happened in science fiction, not in reality. I was still in a state of shock and disbelief over what Steve had done, that would be enough to make the imagination run riot. It could all be explained in a perfectly logical way. Or so I thought. But how could I explain, or put logic to what happened later?

As I unpacked my groceries something fell from my bag onto the kitchen floor. Something that vaguely resembled a spray of white heather. This was real. This was no coincidence. As I bent to retrieve the faded flower, an image of the old lady I had bought it from flashed before my eyes. She was smiling at me. A reassuring smile that told me all would be well. In that moment I knew I could be strong. Steve was gone but life would go on. I would go on. Moving forward day by day until I found the happiness that awaited me somewhere in the not-too-distant future.

BILLY JAMES
F Davies

Candyfloss clouds were the only interruption in the bright blue sky. Beneath them was the hustle and bustle of everyday life carrying on regardless. People always found a way of ignoring the bad things that were happening and sometimes the good things as well. The city was buzzing; it was a bank holiday. Practically everybody had the day off work. The children dragged their parents around the shops trying to squeeze extra gifts out of them, and the elderly took time to sit on park benches and let the breeze blow them down memory lane. It was a day when anything could happen and anything was possible.

Nothing was likely to happen, however, that would induce Billy James Coralis to leave the bench on the sea front. Billy would sit in the same seat every day of the week, rain or shine, without fail. This seat, the one situated closest to the pier was Billy's and had been for a very long time. Not for him was the greenery of the park or the pushing and rushing of the crowded shopping areas. Here he could lean back, close his eyes and listen to the crashing of the waves as they smashed against the timber supports of the pier head, supports that defied the fury of the venomous sea. Sometimes the strains of the music being played by the orchestra that was performing at the Pier Theatre drifted on the air and he would smile wanly as if perhaps remembering snatches of the Prelude in E Sharp Minor.

Daydreaming, he lived again the days and nights of the past, of days when he was young, really young, and the love and laughter of his married life.

Sometimes he would rise quickly to his feet and look intently at someone who was approaching the seat, only to sit again with an air of disappointment and sadness.

Perhaps it was the sound of his name, Coralis, that made some people think that there was a bit of Greek in his ancestry. In fact the only resemblance to anything Greek about him was he was idiosyncratic - from the Greek. His idiosyncrasy was that he only sat on 'his' seat if the tide was coming in.

The people that knew Billy were friendly enough. Some of them on seeing him sitting there would call out to him, 'Here again Billy?' or perhaps, 'You're still here then?'

'Sometimes he would answer with 'I'm waiting for someone' or, 'I have to meet somebody.' Sometimes he wouldn't utter a word. No one believed him. No one had ever seen him there if the tide was out, and no one ever asked him why he only sat there when it was in the ascendancy. That was Billy's secret.

The story began a long time ago . . .

The young man striding the promenade suddenly stopped and began reading the information printed on the large billboard. The information revealed that the music of Liszt and Rachmaninov could be heard at the Pier Theatre. Tickets were on sale from Monday, July 4th. Performances, one daily and for one week only. He made mental notes and turned quickly to move away - 'Oops, sorry, very sorry,' he said to the woman with the most beautiful blue eyes he had ever seen.

'So am I,' she answered with an accent delightful to listen to but hard to distinguish. Scandinavian, possibly. 'Will it stain?' she asked pointing to the generous portion of ice cream that was adorning the breast of his blazer.

'And what about your shoes?' he remarked by way of an answer. A lot of the ice cream cone that she had been about to enjoy was now added decoration on her suede footwear. She uttered a loud expletive that did not sound very ladylike, even though it was spoken in a foreign language. The man broke a very lengthy silence by saying, 'Look, my place is just at the end of the block and I can wash them and this sun will dry them in no time.' Again there was a long silence. 'Please let me help,' he pleaded. She hesitated for a while, 'Make up your mind please,' he said a little impatiently. 'I may just save my jacket,' he added whilst attempting to smile.

'Oh! Alright but I can't wait about for very long. I have to be at the Pier Theatre at 4 o'clock.'

They were at his place in moments. She removed her shoes in the hallway and handed them to him. 'Go on through, make yourself at home,' he invited. 'I won't be long' and off he went to the garden.

Left alone she wandered from room to room and in the last one, the smallest room of them all she was a little surprised to find a piano with the lid open and sheets of music in abundance - most of them on the floor. Picking them up, one at a time and reading them, prompted her to choose one and place it on the piano, all the others she returned to the table from whence they had fallen. Sitting at the piano she struck one or two notes and, after flexing her fingers, she began to play. With eyes closed she was lost to everything but the music she was creating by the magnificence of her playing.

A voice interrupted her. 'Sergei Rachmaninov,' he said. 'The Rhapsody on a Theme of Paganini,' he added.

She looked around, speaking excitedly, 'You know it! You play? Come, come, sit,' and she patted the seat alongside her.

'Yes I know it and I play it, but very badly and you have to go, remember?'

She looked at her watch. 'It is an . . .'

'Who is it, your boyfriend, fiancé, the 4 o'clock date?' he interrupted.

She countered with, 'Did you manage to save your blazer?' and almost in the same breath, 'Are my shoes ready?'

He brought them to her and she closed the piano lid.

She pushed her feet into the slip-ons, 'Thank you, er, er . . .'

'Billy. Just Billy, that will do fine, and you are?' he asked.

She totally ignored the question and replied, 'No, it is not my boyfriend. I have no fiancé.' She looked at her watch again. 'I must go then, thank you for your help,' and pointed to her feet.

'Please, who are you? Your name?'

She paused for a long time. 'Helene. Helle, just Helle, that will do fine.'

'That's one hell of a name Helle.' And for the first time since they had met she smiled broadly at something he had said. They walked to the door, Billy offered his hand.

'Goodbye Billy,' and she was walking away.

On impulse he shouted after her, 'Can we meet again Helle?'

Without turning she called back, loud and clear, 'I have no boy friend. My date is with the Philharmonic at the Pier. I'm auditioning 'The Prelude'.'

Billy strode after her, 'Come back after your audition. Let me know how you got on.' He was rattling away nineteen to the dozen. 'Please come back afterwards, I must see you again Helle.'

She walked a dozen yards or so and with an almost imperceptible wave of her hand shouted 'I'll see what happens . . .'

July 4th saw Helene off on her travels again. The year was 1938 and she had been staying at Billy's on and off since the day they had met exactly a year ago to the day.

Her musical prowess had ensured her a bright and successful career as a concert pianist, but something of a sad and lonely life as it meant spending many weeks away from home and away from her beloved Billy. Her audition had been the stepping stone to the kind of life that neither one of them could have envisaged. She was here, there and everywhere and he missed her so much. When he was alone he could smell her perfume, he could see her long, blonde hair swirling in the breeze. He missed everything about her and she missed him. They were in love. He could hear her quaint magical voice saying, 'Don't worry Billy James, I'll be there with you when the tide comes in. I will always come back to you, darling, I promise.'

The last time she had left to go on tour Billy had taken her to the station. 'Come on BJ, give me a smile,' she had said.

'Promise you will come back, Helle. Don't let anyone steal your heart.'

'Oh! Billy J. I love you so much. I will always be yours. I came back to you after my audition, didn't I? And I will always return to you no matter what happens.'

They had kissed, then she was gone again.

It was nearly October before they were able to spend more time together. In a quiet corner of the local inn they held hands and Billy asked Helle to marry him. 'Of course I will, Billy. I've been waiting so long for you to ask me.'

A delighted, excited Billy asked, 'Soon, very soon Helle?'

And they began to plan the future. She would be away before Christmas for two weeks, then after the holiday they would get married. They laughed happily and recalled the day they first met - the ice cream, the shoes, her four o'clock date.

'I never ever thought for a minute that I would see you again. I was amazed when you came back that evening,' said Billy.

'But very happy if I remember rightly,' Helle said with a wide smile.

Only a dozen or so friends attended their wedding in the early spring of '39 and Helene had toured only once. Since that happy day, life was idyllic. They were pals, mates, lovers bonded for eternity.

They wandered the country lanes, walked the sea front, stopping to read notice boards whilst eating ice creams - with great care, and vowing to love each other for evermore.

Over Europe, however, clouds were forming. Black clouds of war that were drifting swiftly and surely and casting grave doubt in their lives, stifling their happiness and plunging them into an abyss of despair. The climax came in September of that year when Prime Minister Chamberlain broadcast the news to the nation that Britain was at war with Germany.

'Well! Helle Retz. What do we do now girl?' Billy waited for an answer that was not immediate.

'We will know soon enough. It could be difficult for me, I'm not exactly British am I?' was the response.

'But your papers have been finalised. Everything is in order and has been for a long time.'

'Maybe so, Billy, but if you are called up, and no doubt you will be, then tongues will start wagging for sure.'

They talked long into the night and Helle became adamant that she would volunteer to join the forces or any other organisation that would ensure her participation in the war effort against the tyranny of Hitler. Billy wasn't too keen and it showed.

'But I have to. Surely you can see that, Billy?' A long pause then, 'I will be alright, I'll come home safely I promise.'

His call to the colours was quicker than expected and before Christmas they were parted again. The parting was sad and emotional. Locked in each other's arms she whispered, 'Until the tide comes in, Billy. Take care . . . '

Helle was saying goodbye to the elderly relations of her husband who were going to keep an eye on things during the couple's absence. 'Treat the place as your own. Keep it lived in,' were her parting words.

The day's mail was delivered just as she was leaving the house:

Dear Helle,

I am alright, just about, but for obvious reasons I am unable to tell you where we are moving on to. My guess is that we will be gone from here within a day or so. If I am able to write again, I will. God bless, Helle. Happy landings, see you on the tide.   Billy   xxx

With misty eyes she left their home and moved on to the unknown. Her prowess as a brilliant musician had ensured her a position with the forces' entertainment party - concert performers of all sorts and of the highest calibre who were prepared to face danger themselves and travel anywhere in the world to lift the morale of the fighting forces.

A contingent of one such group of artists were standing at the ship's rails. Helle was lounging on deck and composing her husband's letter. Coming to the ending of it she wrote:

Maybe in a few weeks time I will be sunning myself somewhere overseas. I love you very, very much and I always will. No matter what happens, I'll meet you at the seat when the tide is coming in. Don't get your feet wet, Billy. All my love Helle. xxx

She was just sticking the flap of the envelope down when there was a tremendous thump, a blinding flash, then the sickening tearing sound of metal below the waterline parting company. Surprisingly, casualties were light and the occupants of the lifeboats and floats were picked up and taken on board the U-boat. Showing a humane nature, the submarine commander picked up as many survivors as possible - mainly women, one of whom was Helene. These so-called prisoners of war were interned in Germany for a while and after the fall of France taken there, only to be moved again later on. Months of captivity turned into years. Helle was in a way luckier than most of the other internees, for apart from the very occasional Red Cross parcels she shared with the others, her musical prowess enabled her to earn extra rations of food and chocolate as reward for her performances when 'invited' to entertain the high-ranking officers of the German command.

The entertainment evenings were frequent and she was secretly pleased whenever she was ordered to play for them. The piano 'practice' was food and drink to her. It kept her mind sound and her body strong throughout her captivity . . .

Billy sat on that seat for the next few weeks after his homecoming. The sad, lonely weeks became months and summer faded into autumn again. Then the cold of the winter hit them with its bitter north easterly winds and the sea lashed the pier with an added fury. Sea front cafes, ice cream parlours, novelty and stick of rock shops were long since closed, and only people walking their dogs could be seen on the promenade.

The man sitting on the bench near to the pier rose and stamped his feet somewhat gingerly. Then leaning back in his seat, his gloved hands pulled his coat collar tightly around his neck. This coldness, this agony, was nothing compared to the joy and ecstasy that would be his once his darling had returned safely home to him.

He must have fallen asleep. He had been listening to snatches of 'Red Sails in the Sunset' coming from the theatre, the only establishment that was still open. The angry sea still spat and snarled and the wind blew worse than ever. Yet above it all he could hear it so plainly:

'Billy. Billy James. Is it really you?'

Was he dreaming?

'Billy!' He heard his name again and opened his eyes.

There she was! 'Oh, Helle. Helle darling.' Tears blinded him, real salty tears as he held her close. Then she cried and scolded him for not wearing warmer clothes. He looked again in disbelief. 'Is it really you?'

Her answer was, 'Told you that I would come back to you safely, didn't I? Come on Billy, let's go home,' and the seafront roared at them as if it was cheering . . .

TIME WAITS FOR NO MAN
Robert Fallon

Candyfloss clouds were the only interruption in the bright blue sky. Beneath them was the hustle and bustle of everyday life carrying on regardless. People always found a way of ignoring the bad things that were happening and sometimes the good things as well. The city was buzzing; it was a bank holiday. Practically everybody had the day off work. The children dragged their parents around the shops trying to squeeze extra gifts out of them, and the elderly took time to sit on park benches and let the breeze blow them down memory lane. It was a day when anything could happen and anything was possible.

Rob Martin stood on the balcony of his hotel room, four storeys up in the Spanish holiday resort of Lloret. It was his first holiday abroad for 24 years and his first on his own since his divorce. The feeling of isolation at East Midlands airport after a decade and half with wife and children by his side left him feeling hesitant and uneasy. The speed and steep ascent of the jet's take-off had taken him by surprise, thrusting him into a state of panic against the back of his seat. His last flight to Lloret had been in an ageing prop job, with the rivets rattling as it built up power on the runway for a slow, cumbersome take-off. The memories of that journey and holiday in the late 1950s came flooding back.

A bus trip from Leicester to a small airport south of London. The drone of the plane's engines as it made its way to an isolated airstrip on the French border, followed by a terrifying ride in an ancient bus over the mountains into Spain. The journey from Leicester, including a minor bus breakdown, had taken 24 hours. Lloret was a fishing village with a clean, sandy beach almost void of tourists, occupied by fishermen tending their boats and nets. Hotel waitresses were lined up on the seafront ready to carry the guests' luggage to the hotel rooms, which were situated down narrow side streets adjacent to the front. The holiday cost him 38 guineas for a fortnight, equivalent to four weeks' wages, with free bottles of local wine at mealtimes.

He had travelled with two pals, Drew and Pete. Drew was a born romantic with an easy-going nature and Pete a no-frills guy with a dry sense of humour. They also palled up with two London lads, Max and Terry, on the trip out. As fate would have it, they were all on the same hotel wing as two English girls, Joan and Sheila. Drew was soon working on his chat-up lines to Joan, the shy beauty of the two, trying his hardest to impress. It all went horribly wrong for Drew a couple of days later when he trotted to the communal toilet in high spirits. It was situated at the end of the short corridor, in full view of Pete as he rested on his bed with the room door open to let in some much-needed fresh air. Joan made her way to the toilet. Unfortunately Drew, in a dreamy state, had not locked the door and found himself staring open-mouthed at Joan with his shorts round his ankles. Without a word, Joan fled to her room in a state of shock. When Drew finally made an embarrassed appearance, he found Pete rolling about hysterically on the bedroom floor. After a gusty apology to the blushing Joan, the romance took off again.

Two nights later, as a party of them walked along the promenade, Drew took Joan by the hand, walked down the beach to the water's edge and swept her dramatically into his arms. A freak wave swept up the beach, engulfing them both. Drew, in a light grey suit and suede shoes, took it all in his stride, consoling the spluttering Joan. You just could not fault the guy for his endurance. His misfortunes made Pete's holiday an unqualified success. Joan's companion, Sheila, must have been warned about the nightmares virile young men can bestow on young ladies as it was difficult to get her face to relax into a smile. He himself had pushed his luck with a blonde 35-year-old divorcee who had joined their party. Sadly, she was not interested in being bedded by a toy boy, one named Rob in particular. They all met up regularly at a six-lane wooden skittles alley, with young Spanish lads replacing the skittles and rolling the woods back for a few pesetas. The alley also contained a small bar and dancing area. It was an oasis in acres of land, planted with olive trees which were draped in fairy lights around the alley. The owners had a teenage daughter who served behind the bar. Max was smitten as soon as he set eyes on her, spending his holiday googoo-eyed at the bar. Terry tried to tell him he was wasting his time as it was difficult to date a Spanish girl then, without her mother or granny tagging along as chaperone.

With over a week of his return holiday to Lloret gone, he was still amazed at the change from olive trees and empty sands to towering hotels and crowded beaches. At first he found it difficult to get his bearings as most of the long-remembered landmarks were long gone.

He was staying at the Flamenco Hotel in the heart of Lloret with his balcony, in a side street, facing the rows of balconies of a neighbouring hotel 20 feet away. Sleep was impossible from midnight until dawn. 'Flower of Scotland' to 'Land of my Fathers' echoed across the street. Exhibitionists had a field day from the safety of their balconies. Most were not a pretty sight! The sangria was flowing in abundance with the hotel corridors sounding like echo chambers. If a door slammed shut, it vibrated through every room on the floor. Top of the bill in the early morning entertainment was a character named Princess Sheba who was a dark-skinned 20-stoner dressed in colourful, flowing robes. Sheba was married to a redheaded Welshman named Barry, with six kids aged five to twelve in tow. The kids ran wild and were all addicted to the ciggies. Sheba and the slightly built Barry saw life through a permanent alcoholic haze. They enjoyed telling all and sundry that Sheba belonged to the Royal Family of Tonga. She would make a dramatic entrance on their balcony, with her screaming backing group, just after midnight. For hours on end she would rant and rave about the English swine, lager louts and whores to all within hearing distance. Witty and angry comments about Tonga cannibals, Welsh sheep-lovers and who had fathered her brood, would rebound on her like a torrent. Although tiresome, it was all quite entertaining - a street theatre from a wild species of life.

On the second night of his holiday, as he stood outside his hotel, he happened to glance across the wide main street and could not believe his eyes. Almost opposite, hidden between towering hotels, was the small entrance to the old skittle alley, lit up by a few fairy lights which were insignificant amongst the flashing neon signs of the hotels, nightclubs and arcades. With mixed feelings he made his way towards it, wondering if the young daughter could have possibly kept it going, as he still had a picture of her framed in his mind. To his surprise her parents were still there serving behind the bar at the side of the unchanged skittle alley. Apart from a few added laughter lines, they were exactly as he remembered them. 'Excuse me,' he asked, 'do you have a daughter in her late thirties or early forties?'

'Yes,' they replied, 'why do you ask?'

He explained how he had been to Lloret and frequented the alley 24 years ago and did they remember a young Londoner named Max who was infatuated with their daughter?

'Well, we should remember,' said the smiling dad. 'Max came back as often as possible and eventually they got married and set up home in London. Our grandson is coming over for a working holiday at the weekend. We are having a party and you are invited.'

The party was a sumptuous affair where we met Don, the image of his dad, Max. He told the lad of his dad's wasted holiday. Don laughed, saying, 'Wait till I get back home. I won't half pull his leg.'

It had been an enjoyable and unforgettable experience, party and all. Max had married into a fortune from the acres of land sold off for development. The parents kept the profitable business on, as that was their way of life. Their priorities were spot on.

It was approaching midday when, above the noise rising from the busy street below, he heard a loud argument coming from the room of the Welsh 'Rarebits' across the street. The large figure of Princess Sheba staggered onto their balcony with the small figure of hubby Barry clinging on her back, one arm in a strangle-hold across her throat. Barry, from a combination of booze, loud-mouthed Sheba, six snotty kids and the hot sun, had finally snapped. He clung on grimly as the scream became choked in Sheba's throat and she slumped down in an unconscious heap. Rob gave a sigh of relief. Tonight he might get some sleep.

THE MESSAGE
F Jensen

Candyfloss clouds were the only interruption in the bright blue sky. Beneath them was the hustle and bustle of everyday life carrying on regardless. People always found a way of ignoring the bad things that were happening and sometimes the good things as well. The city was buzzing; it was a bank holiday. Practically everybody had the day off work. The children dragged their parents around the shops trying to squeeze extra gifts out of them, and the elderly took time to sit on park benches and let the breeze blow them down memory lane. It was a day when anything could happen and anything was possible.

Pam and Jeff had chosen a quiet part of the beach on which to spend the afternoon. They had found somewhere to relax in the shade while their ten-year-old twins Matthew and Gary entertained themselves at the water's edge.

Matthew was searching for crabs and Gary was throwing pebbles at a shiny object bobbing about on the incoming tide. To him it was an enemy submarine, a U-boat no less, and he was determined to keep it at bay. After many unsuccessful throws there was a faint pinging sound and he shouted, 'Got it! What a great shot. A bullseye I reckon.'

Matthew looked out, shading his eyes. 'What is it? What have you hit?' There was a momentary glint in the water.

'It's over there,' Gary said, pointing. 'Look it's a bottle of some sort.'

They both paddled out to get a better look and the water was soon up to their knees. They hesitated, aware of the steeply sloping beach and the fast incoming tide, even though the bottle was now tantalisingly close.

'Let's leave it,' suggested Matthew, the cautious one. 'It's only a bottle.'

But Gary's adventurous nature asserted itself. 'No, we must get it. There might be a message in it,' he said hopefully.

Matthew was already wading back to shallower water when a wave, larger than most, swept the bottle briefly within reach. Gary was ready for it and snatched it out of the water, holding it aloft like a trophy. 'I've got it,' he shouted triumphantly, splashing his way back to Matthew's side. 'and wow, there's something inside it - just like I said.'

Together, they examined it and after much pulling and twisting succeeded in removing the cork together with the contents - a rolled up piece of paper. Gary carefully unrolled it and read out its message, with Matthew looking over his shoulder. 'Please help to secure our release,' it said. 'You will need the password which can be obtained from the manager of your nearest supermarket. Please hurry. There will be a reward.'

Gary's mind was racing. 'They must be held captive in some foreign country,' he said darkly. 'and they've slipped the bottle into the sea when no-one was watching.'

'Or else it's been thrown overboard from a ship,' Matthew suggested. 'Let's take it to mum and dad, they'll know what to do.'

They raced back to where their parents were savouring this rare spell of solitude, Pam reading a paperback and Jeff , eyes closed and half asleep.

'Look what we've found,' shouted Matthew, excitedly, 'It's a bottle with a message in it.'

Jeff sat up with a start. 'Let me see it,' he said, almost snatching at the note.

He read it aloud to Pam and she was quick to spot an obvious anomaly. 'What on earth has a supermarket got to do with bringing about someone's release?' she pondered.

Jeff shook his head. 'The whole thing seems very odd. It's not even hand-written, he pointed out, it's printed. It doesn't seem like a genuine cry for help to me. Let's make for the nearest supermarket and see if they can solve the mystery.'

In the manager's office at the supermarket, Jeff produced the note and asked the manager if he could shed any light on it.

'I certainly can,' he said with a smile. 'It's the third I've seen this week.'

'Is there really a password involved?' Jeff asked

'Oh yes. The magic word is *Zippo.* That's the name of the soft drinks company that's organised this publicity stunt. It's aiming to break into the lucrative soft drinks market and it's certainly generating a lot of interest.'

'And where are the bottles being launched from? Somewhere on the French coast do you think?'

'Oh no. They're released from the bay, just around the corner. Apparently they drop one in at each change of tide.'

'So it's not a cry for help then,' said Jeff, with a laugh.

'Not at all, it's a cry to sample their new brand of soft drink.'

Jeff thanked him and turned to go when Gary tugged his sleeve.

'Ask him about the reward,' he hissed.

The manager overheard him and stood up. 'Of course, I'm sorry, I forgot.' He picked up the phone and spoke to someone. Then he turned to Jeff: 'If you wait by the door, John will carry it out to your car for you.' He shook their hands and they made their way out.

John joined them at the door, carrying a plain cardboard carton which obviously contained something heavy. He walked with them to the car, eased the carton into the boot and straightened up. 'Your reward, sir,' he said. Gary eyed the mysterious carton with great interest and Jeff felt he had to ask the obvious question. 'What is it?' he enquired. John looked surprised at the question. 'It's a dozen trial-size bottles of Zippo,' he said.

CANDYFLOSS DREAMS
Ise Obomhense

Candyfloss clouds were the only interruption in the bright blue sky.
Beneath them was the hustle and bustle of everyday life carrying on
regardless. People always found a way of ignoring the bad things that
were happening and sometimes the good things as well. The city was
buzzing; it was a bank holiday. Practically everybody had the day off
work. The children dragged their parents around the shops trying to
squeeze extra gifts out of them, and the elderly took time to sit on park
benches and let the breeze blow them down memory lane. It was a day
when anything could happen and anything was possible.

Jenna had thought long and hard, coming to the decision that she
could no longer live in this house, it had too many bad memories for
her. She had seen her mother die in this house and all her childhood
dreams shattered. Her mother had been her whole world while growing
up. Kelly Matthews was kind and considerate, as well as being
beautiful. As a child Jenna had idolized her mother and wanted to be
like her. She even tried to dress like her and copied her mannerisms;
thus all good things must come to an end. Everything started to change
when Jenna was in her early teens. Kelly Matthews changed from the
attentive, loving mother to an unhappy woman who drank too much.
Jenna's mother's drinking was the cause of all the arguments at home,
which eventually led to her parents splitting up. The day Jake Matthews
packed his bags and left, was the day that his daughter had to grow up
overnight.

Jenna had to learn to fend for herself. Her mother had no interest in
her and her father made no attempt to keep in touch. Jenna was alone
for the first time. It was hard for Jenna being a teenager with no one to
support and comfort her. Jenna found solace in her studies and buried
herself in her work. She hoped to get accepted to a top university.
Unfortunately, that dream was also destroyed by the fact that her
mother became ill as a result of years of alcohol abuse. With no one to
take care of her, Jenna had to stay at home and look after her mom. For
three years Jenna watched her mother slowly deteriorate, till there was
nothing left of the woman she once loved and respected. How cruel life
can be. Kelly Matthews spent her life looking after other people - her
husband, her daughter - until she could give no more. She turned to the

bottle for comfort and as a result, poisoned her liver, damaging it beyond repair.

It's funny how life turns out. Three years after making the decision to stay and look after her mother, Jenna was still in the same house, but this time she was packing to leave. Leaving a home that had been a significant part of her life. Many memories were shared, some good and some bad. She was now approaching the end of an era. Walking out of the door with her bags packed gave Jenna a new lease of life - a sense of freedom. The past was finally behind her.

Jenna handed her things to her boyfriend, Greg. 'Are you ready?'

'I have been ready for a long time, Greg.'

As they were about to get into their car, Jenna heard someone call out to her to wait. It was her father. Jenna had heard that Jake Matthews was back in town, but she figured he wouldn't try to make contact with her as he had not in the past.

'Jenna, wait. We need to talk. I've been waiting for ages.'

'So have I, Dad. In fact it has been way too long and now I have nothing to say to you.'

'I might not have been there for you in the past, but I am here now.'

'I will bear that in mind, Dad.' Jenna turned to Greg and signalled to him, letting him know that she was now ready to leave. They got in the car and set off. Jenna suddenly realized that she didn't even know when she might see her father next, but life is unpredictable and anything can happen. She wasn't looking for someone to love, but she found Greg and he was the one sane thing in her life.

THE DREAM TEAM
E Timmins

Candyfloss clouds were the only interruption in the bright blue sky. Beneath them was the hustle and bustle of everyday life carrying on regardless. People always found a way of ignoring the bad things that were happening and sometimes the good things as well. The city was buzzing; it was a bank holiday. Practically everybody had the day off work. The children dragged their parents around the shops trying to squeeze extra gifts out of them, and the elderly took time to sit on park benches and let the breeze blow them down memory lane. It was a day when anything could happen and anything was possible.

Wee Danny Brown kicked a pebble disconsolately along the pavement. 'No World Cup. No more football for a week or two. No nothing.'

His favourite football heroes, David Beckham and Michael Owen, belonged in another part of the country. He had supported their teams, but could only see them when they were on TV. In the background he heard shouts, but nothing penetrated his deep thoughts. Suddenly it went dark . . .

The cheering had died down long ago, but the feeling of happiness was still in his heart. He had seen David Beckham and Michael Owen on the supporters' bus as they returned home - *heroes.* Yes, he had been a long way from the bus, but the pleasure of being there was almost as good as seeing them, wasn't it? He couldn't remember how he had come here, but who cares?

As he wandered along the streets, nothing was really familiar, but he felt safe and somehow he knew where to go. In the distance two young men were coming towards him and as they drew near, Danny held his breath. It couldn't be, could it?

'Hello Danny,' said David Beckham.

'Hi, how goes it?' Michael Owen joined in.

'How do you know my name,' asked Danny.

'We've heard all about you. We know you enjoy football. You see us on the TV when you can and you have wanted to meet us for a long time.'

Danny held his breath. This couldn't be true.

'There's an ice cream van along the road, would you like one?'

Danny just nodded, absolutely tongue-tied.

As they walked along the street to the ice cream van, David and Michael told Danny how they had been like him, enjoying football since they were young. They had been encouraged by their parents and teachers and had practised very hard.

As they approached the van, Danny's eyes opened very wide. 'No, it can't be true. I must be dreaming.'

'Hello, Danny, which kind would you like?'

Danny couldn't say a word. He just stared. Michael answered the man selling the ice cream. 'We'll all have a large cone with a flake, please.'

With eyes still popping, Danny took the ice cream from Michael and as he paid the money, Michael said, 'Thanks, Boss.' They waved their goodbyes and carried on along the road, enjoying their ice creams. David and Michael carried on talking to Danny, but all he could think of was the ice cream man and David and Michael. His three football heroes. Wasn't he lucky? He'd be the envy of every other child living.

Danny had just finished his ice cream as he felt himself falling. Two arms held him tightly. 'Are you alright, son?'

Danny looked up into the doctor's face. He nodded his head. 'Where are David and Michael and . . . '

'He seems a bit delirious, but I can't find anything broken. We'll keep him in the hospital for a day or two, but he seems OK.'

Danny heard his mother's voice and suddenly he knew he was OK. Then he heard his father's voice which reassured him further.

'The scaffolding of the building you were passing collapsed. No one was injured and you were very lucky.'

Danny agreed. He would tell them how lucky he had been. He would tell them of his wonderful meeting with the three great football heroes when he returned home. He couldn't wait to see their faces.

MIRACLES DO HAPPEN
Lorna Moffatt

Candyfloss clouds were the only interruption in the bright blue sky. Beneath them was the hustle and bustle of everyday life carrying on regardless. People always found a way of ignoring the bad things that were happening and sometimes the good things as well. The city was buzzing; it was a bank holiday. Practically everybody had the day off work. The children dragged their parents around the shops trying to squeeze extra gifts out of them, and the elderly took time to sit on park benches and let the breeze blow them down memory lane. It was a day when anything could happen and anything was possible.

Doreen decided to take her sandwiches and flask of tea into Hyde Park on her day off work and eat them on one of the seats facing the Serpentine. She could then feed the birds at the same time. She was rather a plain girl who had never made the most of herself. Long, straight brown hair tied back, horn-rimmed glasses and flat shoes did nothing for her appearance at all.

She could see on the other side of the lake a crowd of people near some parked vans, cameras on trolleys and campers all illuminated with arc lights. She wondered why they would need extra lights to make a film when the natural sunlight today was so strong that she had to replace her spectacles with sunglasses.

The sound of the crowd clapping wafted across the lake in the still of the sunny day.

Chapter Two:

Godfrey Hurst bent across his leading lady who scowled up at him and made a sarcastic comment under her breath. They hated each other. He wished that this interminable film was finished and he could get away from his once-upon-a-time girlfriend. She had been playing the prima donna in this one all right. That was the reason they were filming on a bank holiday instead of sitting on a beach somewhere. He wished he could wash this melting make-up off his tired face and have a long, cool drink sitting on the grass under the trees. One of the cameras made a popping noise and then a stream of smoke came from the top.

'Cut,' yelled the director. 'Take a break. Ten minutes, no more,' and he crossed to talk to the camera man.

Godfrey jumped away from his pouting leading lady and ran round the back of the vans to where he had seen the trees. He flopped down on a patch of grass.

'Don't you get grass stains on them trousers,' nagged a passing continuity girl with her clipboard sticking to her hot arm.

He ignored her, looking up at the sunlight making bright stars through the leaves of the trees.

'Another half hour,' a voice said at his elbow. 'You'll have to try and appease her, Godfrey,' added the director. 'You know she thinks she's the star and she's nothing but a spent nova. Try and get her moving along. We are never going to get this film finished, it's already over budget.' He walked over to the camera crew who were transferring their half-made film to another camera.

Godfrey lay right back on the grass, daydreaming about his life in the film industry and the bad tempered 'star'. He had first fallen in love with acting at the school Christmas play and from that day on wanted to be nothing but an actor. His parents could not afford to send him to acting school, so he paid for it himself, working as an office boy in the building society to earn his keep and pay his fees.

He thought about the long line of girlfriends he had had. Far too cunning was Godfrey to actually marry any of them. Phew, he thought, thank goodness I never proposed marriage to Gloria Sampson, the 'star'. After his former girlfriends, she had seemed so glamorous. With the then famous Miss Sampson on his arm, he was accepted at all the right parties and found no trouble at all getting the best tables in the booked restaurants. It was after moving into her smart flat in Kensington that the disillusion set in; after she removed the bounteous blonde hair and pealed off the artificial eyelashes. Watching her remove the layers of make-up from a lined and pale face with enough cream for a hospital, he started to realise she was a sham. He kept up the pretence. There were compensations: there was the money and then the introductions. In the beginning she had been amiable enough, but as the daily number of glasses of wine increased, so did her temper tantrums. This would be the last film she would make with him, he vowed. Anyway, he was the 'star' of this film and was making his own way in the world now. He did not need her. To where though, he thought. Was he going to end up like a beached whale in some rundown seaside town, boring the other drinkers in some scruffy bar with tales of his exploits as a film star?

The director paused beside him again. 'You can lie there all day if you want, we can't use just one camera. Filming is over for the day. Five o'clock start tomorrow,' and he sauntered away, puffing on a large cigar and not waiting for a reply.

Funny, thought Godfrey, how his cigars get bigger with his overdraft.

Godfrey was very comfortable on the grass, lying in the sun in Hyde Park. He decided he would stay there at least for a while and recap on his life, starting with his girlfriends.

Right at the beginning on his first day in the building society, there had been the girl on the switchboard. Godfrey had always been a handsome chap and never had any difficulty attracting the opposite sex. What was her name, he thought? She had been kind to him all the time he worked in the building society and was never jealous when he took other girls to the pictures. She knew she was not much to look at. But then, she had been nice, with lovely skin. His thoughts went over at least ten other girlfriends, some nice, some beautiful, but every so often his thoughts returned to her. Doreen, that was her name, he thought. I last saw her the day she bought that old banger of a car. She had been on about getting a car to take her crippled mother out for rides in the country because she was housebound. Then when the day came, she collected it in the lunch hour and what was it? A beat up old Morris Countryman. Poor Doreen, I was rotten to her.

It was getting very hot and he was thirsty, so he sauntered over to the hospitality van, collected a Coke and roved off around the Serpentine until he came to a seat where there was space to sit down. A woman of about his age was already sitting there and he asked her permission to sit down.

'Of course,' she said taking off her sun glasses and looking straight up at him.

'Doreen,' he exclaimed in surprise.

'Yes, fancy you remembering my name and you a famous film star and all that. I've got a scrap book on you, I've followed your career all along.' Godfrey was amazed. He sat down with a thump and the seat bounced up and down. 'Not as little as I used to be.' He felt just as he had that first day he met her, with his too-big new shirt and carefully tied building society tie, being jostled by a bevy of hefty girls. Then she had come to his rescue and here she was again. Before he could stop himself he said, 'I remember you all right on the switchboard of the building society and are you still taking your mum out in that old Morris C . . ?' He stopped. Her face went red and her eyes clouded over.

'Mum used to like to go out in my car, it never lets me down you know.'

'Sorry,' he said and the first thing he could think of, 'those cars are classic you know. You said 'used to'.'

'Mum died last year. I'm on my own now and I'm not on the switchboard anymore, I'm head of personnel.'

'Quite right too, I can't think of anyone better,' he replied, trying to reprieve himself. 'You said 'it never lets me down,' have you still got it then?'

'Oh yes, Mum said it suits me, I would be out of place in anything else.'

'No you wouldn't Doreen. You don't belong in an old Morris Countryman at all, in my estimation, you belong in that,' he said, pointing to his stretched white Limousine parked beside the filming vans, 'and what's more you're going out in it to lunch, for starters, that is. Now we'll give those birds your cheese sandwiches and off we go.'

Miracles do happen in the most unlikely places.

SECOND CHANCE
Gillian Mullett

Candyfloss clouds were the only interruption in the bright blue sky. Beneath them was the hustle and bustle of everyday life carrying on regardless. People always found a way of ignoring the bad things that were happening and sometimes the good things as well. The city was buzzing; it was a bank holiday. Practically everybody had the day off work. The children dragged their parents around the shops trying to squeeze extra gifts out of them, and the elderly took time to sit on park benches and let the breeze blow them down memory lane. It was a day when anything could happen and anything was possible.

It was a day when anything could happen and anything was possible from good fortune to disaster. About two miles outside of the town, that is if you cut across the fields, or longer by the well worn unsurfaced road, used years past by many lorries, hidden low down and looking like a volcano's crater, lay the abandoned quarry.

The water that had filled the bottom over time, lay there dark and still like a great open mouth ready to swallow, anyone that dared to encroach upon its foreboding surface.

Although fenced off it was no deterrent to the local boys who frequently visited the site. Mainly because they had been told it was dangerous and out of bounds.

This warning was enough to stir their imaginations and urge their need for exploration, not to mention sheer defiance.

James Ashley Russell or Jamie to his friends, had the reputation of being fearless when it came to fights and always the first to try anything with risk involved to increase his reputation and standing with *his gang.*

After all he was the boss, head of the gang and at the youthful age of twelve years was always looking for ways to show and keep his supremacy.

That lovely summer day Jamie gathered his gang together, they were always complaining of being bored and looked with relish to their meetings.

Daniel was Number 2 in the gang and woe betide anyone that called him Dan, he always maintained that he was named after Daniel who fought the lions. Stretching the accuracy of his story didn't matter not when you are Number 2.

Then there was Robby a great football enthusiast, forever bouncing and kicking a ball and always boasting that he would one day play in the World Cup.

Robby was a few months older than Jamie, but it was never mentioned.

Finally there was Luke. He was a real whiz with the computer and the gang relied heavily on him when it came to homework.

Luke always thought situations through and never took chances, some regarded him as a little slow, others could see the potential that lay ahead of him.

It was hard to see why Luke wanted to be in a gang, but he was sure that it was this that had made the bullies at school leave him well alone.

After they had exchanged their greetings that were never more than *whatcha* or *ok* or even *alright mate,* Jamie suggested a visit to the quarry. No one ever disagreed with him, not that they were scared, but that they could never come up with any better idea.

So off they set climbing over fences, kicking anything that lay in their path on the ground, and talking over their exploits in the past.

When the quarry came into sight they all started to run as Jamie had just put out the challenge that the last to slide down the crater was yellow.

So they all grabbed a large piece of cardboard that they had taken there on another occasion. They sat on it at the top of the very steep sloping sides and then like people on a sledge in winter's snow took off. They tried to control their speed by digging in their heels into the dirt and stones with clouds of dry sand clouding over them.

They all screamed at the top of their voices, as they knew that they should not even be there, but this made it all the more exciting and as their hearts banged in their chest they could see Jamie well in front of all of them. When he put the challenge down it was always because he knew that he would win and this time was not going to be any different.

All the gang started to slow down as they reached closer to the water but not Jamie, he did not intend to be the loser.

The sides of the quarry came to an abrupt stop at the water's edge, there was no levelling out so Jamie was catapulted with his cardboard straight into the muddy, cold and very, very deep water. Jamie could not swim but had made sure that the gang would never find out as they may consider this a weakness, and that in a gang leader would never be tolerated.

As the coldness struck Jamie's limbs he started to fight for that had been his answer to everything that he could not control.

He was too far off the bank for anyone to help although his friends kept calling his name and shouting instructions, in a desperate effort to do something for him.

Then the feeling of sheer helplessness stilled their voices.

As Jamie slid from view and the waters closed over him, their hearts sank and they dropped onto the quarry floor exhausted and scared.

Sinking deeper and deeper into the blackness Jamie came to realise the futility of fighting, his arms and legs grew heavier and heavier and colder and colder and he realised the inevitability of his actions.

Then he was suddenly aware of a light, even though his eyes were shut tight and he was still drifting slowly, lower into total darkness.

It passed through his mind of the stones that he and his friend had so often thrown into the water and wondered if he like the stones would never be seen again.

As he felt himself drifting into sleep it seemed that the light followed and totally surrounded him. Then what felt like two great hands supported him, and he finally stopped sinking.

Very gradually he started to rise and as he did he dared to open his eyes.

The light gave him a magnificent sense of peace, warmth and contentment that Jamie felt deep within his heart.

A voice in his head told him not to worry and that everything would be all right.

Then the light and the voice left him and he instinctively knew that he was at the surface. Jamie came up at the last few seconds with such a force that he was expelled from the water gasping for breath and taking in the fresh summer air, it never felt so good.

Luke had already found some rope left by the quarry workers and he hoped with all his might that it would be strong enough to pull Jamie out of his would-be grave.

He need not have worried for strangely - or was it strange? - Jamie was in reaching distance from his friends who grabbed his hands fervently with much relief.

After some considerable time the gang finally recovered enough to start their journey home. Jamie was quite subdued but his friends put that down to his narrow escape and wondering what on earth he would tell his mother about his wet clothes, but then he always thought of something. Jamie went over and over in his mind what had happened, the wonderful beautiful light, the voice that was not his own and wondered if he had actually died.

He had heard of near death experiences and always put them down as fanciful imagination, but now he would have to think again.

If this was not a near death experience what was it?

He though it best not to tell the gang, they might laugh at him and heads of gangs don't like being laughed at.

Jamie knew that he would never forget, and felt sure that guardian angels do exist, but from now on he would find something else for his friends to do and would keep clear of the quarry, for hadn't he been given a second chance?

OVER A BIGMAC
Kristina Howells

Candyfloss clouds were the only interruption in the bright blue sky. Beneath them was the hustle and bustle of everyday life carrying on regardless. People always found a way of ignoring the bad things that were happening and sometimes the good things as well. The city was buzzing; it was a bank holiday. Practically everybody had the day off work. The children dragged their parents around the shops trying to squeeze extra gifts out of them, and the elderly took time to sit on park benches and let the breeze blow them down memory lane. It was a day when anything could happen and anything was possible.

Jenny though found it was a case of looking out for the man of her dreams, whilst sitting dreamily looking out of the window of the crowded McDonald's restaurant eating a BigMac meal. Jenny, a business executive from Leicester had just come back from a rather tiresome journey in London. Not wanting to eat anything on the train, a BigMac meal was something she had longed for since departing London on the 5pm train.

Struggling into the restaurant carrying her big black bag and raincoat, she found the table that was perfect for looking out onto the world passing by. Dumping her stuff on the chair, she went to the counter to order her meal, taking the tray to her table with lots of delicious food on it, before devouring the food and focusing on the world as it passed by. Suddenly, as if time had stood still, she spotted the perfect guy, as he walked through the door of the McDonald's restaurant.

The man, who was somewhat tall in stature, with short brown hair, dressed in the latest designer clothes, carrying a briefcase, was already her idol.

Staring at the vacant seat next to her, she hoped he would sit in it. then just as he had read her mind, the most gorgeous man ever bought his meal to the vacant seat next to her, reading the Racing Post as he ate his meal. Jenny couldn't help but use that as a way of making conversation.

'Err, excuse me,' Jenny said rather coyly, 'do you have the time please?'

'Yes it's 6.45,' he replied softly, with a distinct London accent that she loved to hear.

'Thank you,' she smiled, 'you couldn't tell me who won the main race today, wherever racing had occurred.'

'Oh no! I am looking at tomorrow's entries as my friend has a horse racing tomorrow in Nottingham.'

'Great, well I'm not into racing, I'm more into football. Do you like football?' Jenny asked, hoping that the conversation would not end, and he would turn around to ask her to accompany him to the local pub or for a walk in the park on the way home.

Then, just as he was about to reply to her question, his mobile phone began to ring. She couldn't help but listen in on his conversation as he answered the call. Thinking it could be his wife or his girlfriend, she pretended not to show any disappointment of his attachment as he came off the phone.

'Well I must go,' Jenny politely remarked, after finishing the last chip that was left in the packet, 'I hope your friend's horse runs well.'

'Thank you,' he beamed.

She then got up and put her empty carton and tray on the side. As she did, he quickly reached out to her from behind, and gently touched her arm. 'Would you like to go somewhere for a drink?' he asked quietly, 'but before you say no, I am not married and I did not deliberately ignore your question as I am into football.'

'Great,' she said, 'I would love to accompany you to the pub.'

'Does Yates sound okay?'

'Fine,' she beamed.

They slowly made their way out of McDonald's towards the pub. On the way, they both began to speak of the short synopsis in their own personal history, trying not to tell him too much of her life, she began to bring the subject back to football.

Yet every time he spoke, even when they reached the pub and the drinks had been ordered, she couldn't help but notice his bright blue eyes and the lovely smile that made his enamelled teeth shine, thus making her feel all weak like a jelly sitting underneath ice cream.

'Do you live far?' Jenny asked.

'No, not far.'

'Oh,' she smiled, 'I live with my flat mate called Jessica overlooking the park.'

'Then we must be neighbours,' he exclaimed.

She couldn't believe her luck. Her head was beginning to swirl with delight at this very thought, neighbours.

After several more pints, they soon strolled out of the pub holding hands. A moment of silence passed between them, before he took hold of Jenny, stroking her hair, and hugging her. Then without warning the long awaited kiss had finally arrived. Jenny, wishing that this didn't have to end soon found reality setting in.

As the dark stranger, tall in stature soon broke free and parted company, leaving her stunned in her tracks as the man of her dreams slowly disappeared into the sunset, until he could no longer be seen in view.

Jenny, now on her way home, carrying her big black bag, found herself forgetting all about the hustle and bustle of the day. With just the breeze adding to another memory, down the lane.

BANK HOLIDAY
Ann Madge

Candyfloss clouds were the only interruption in the bright blue sky. Beneath them was the hustle and bustle of everyday life carrying on regardless. People always found a way of ignoring the bad things that were happening and sometimes the good things as well. The city was buzzing; it was a bank holiday. Practically everybody had the day off work. The children dragged their parents around the shops trying to squeeze extra gifts out of them, and the elderly took time to sit on park benches and let the breeze blow them down memory lane. It was a day when anything could happen and anything was possible.

The coach carrying its passengers to the historical city of Plymouth for a day's outing, crawled along the A38.

Brian Markham glanced anxiously at his heavily pregnant wife Sally.

'You alright love?' he enquired cautiously. 'Maybe this wasn't such a good idea after all. I never thought the traffic would be like this.'

Sally shrugged. 'It's the bank holiday Brian,' We'll just have to be patient. Oh look, they seem to be moving on now.'

'He kissed her cheek. 'You're one in a million Sal. I'm a lucky man.'
Shifting her bulk, she grimaced. 'I do wish that woman behind us would cease nagging. Imagine living with that all the time.'

Pensioner Fred Barratt leaned back in his seat and closed his eyes; the chatter of his wife Joan and her sister Flo grating on his nerves. Flo and he had always clashed. Why did she have to tag along anyway? Digging her sister in the ribs, Flo nodded towards Sally.

'Would you look at the size of her? Taking a risk isn't she? I wouldn't venture out if it were me.' Joan pursed her lips.

'Don't be soft our Flo. What she does is her business.'

Len and Vivien Paget, together with their two young children, were beginning to annoy fellow passengers.

'Lisa Paget, give over or I'll slap your legs. Len. Don't just sit there. Look at her scuffing her shoes!'

Glaring at his wife, Len pulled his cap over his eyes. Some trip this was turning out to be. Feeling a dig in his shins, he cuffed young Robert. He had been a fool to agree to this fiasco in the beginning.

The coach eventually arrived in Plymouth an hour behind schedule, and feeling decidedly hot and uncomfortable, Rex Firkin, the driver, glanced at the motley assembly in his mirror. Well at least he'd get to see Pat for a few hours, bless her.

'Well here we are folks,' said Rex thankfully. 'Sorry about the delay, but we'll stay an extra hour to make up for it. If you could all be back here promptly by six pm I'd be grateful. Have a nice day.'

As the passengers alighted, the Barretts began to argue. 'We must have a cream tea Fred,' proclaimed his sister-in-law. 'We've been looking forward to it, haven't we our Joan?'

Sighing with exasperation, Fred glanced at his watch. 'You're daft the pair of you. It's not even lunchtime yet.'

The sisters shrugged indifferently. 'You may join us if you wish then, or do the other,' stated Joan bluntly.

Fred did not hesitate. 'I'll do the other then, if it's all the same to you. See you back at the coach.'

Joan stared after her husband's retreating figure with dismay. 'He's spoilt the day already,' she sighed dispiritedly.

Flo patted her sister's arm. 'Not really,' she laughed gaily. 'Now we can do as we darn well please.'

The Paget family trailed miserably around the bustling city centre, trying to pacify their demanding offspring.

'For goodness sake Viv, buy the little perishers something and then perhaps we'll have some peace,' growled Len. 'Here. This will do. Everything a pound. That can't be bad.'

His wife pursed her lips. 'Oh very well. Then we'll go up on the Hoe and relax. My feet are killing me!'

Len shook his head. 'I told you you'd be sorry for wearing those heels, but as usual you wouldn't listen. Come on then kids. In we go.'

The Markhams had enjoyed a light lunch, although frequently Sally would experience a twinge in her abdomen.

Once again Brian glanced dubiously at his wife. I wish to God we'd stayed at home Sal. You should be relaxing on the bed in the cool. It's so damned hot isn't it?'

She bit her lip. 'I'll be alright Bri. It was rather cramped on the coach. I fancy a bit of sea air. Why don't we stroll up on to the Hoe? There's bound to be somewhere we can sit a while.'

Brian frowned. 'Well if you're sure love.'

But as she rose, Sally blanched. 'Oh Bri. I think my waters have broken!'

Having enjoyed their cream tea and bought a few souvenirs, Joan and Flo were relaxing nearby, when Joan, observing the distraught parents-to-be, grabbed her sister's arm. 'Oh look Flo. She looks in a bad way poor lass. We'd best help.'

Flo merely snorted. 'It's not our problem sister.'

Joan glared at her heartless sibling. 'That's just where you're wrong Flo.' Then rising briskly from her seat, Joan approached the young couple. 'Hello, can I help? We're on the same coach aren't we?'

Tears streaming down her face, Sal gazed fearfully into Joan's compassionate eyes. 'It had to happen here didn't it? The baby's started early. I don't think I can wait until . . . Ahh!'

Joan and Brian exchanged worried glances.

'No you can't my dear,' said Joan flatly. 'You'd best phone an ambulance lad. They've got a phone in that cafe behind us.' She turned to the quivering Sally. 'Sit tight Pet. We'll get you there in good time.'

Fred stirred uneasily as his sister-in-law advanced towards him. 'So here you are Fred Barratt. I might have known you'd be on the hard stuff. Well you'll be pleased to know your wife has poked her oar in.'

Fred glared at the dour-faced woman. 'What exactly do you mean Flo? Explain yourself,' he retorted tartly.

She tutted. 'That pregnant girl. She's gone into labour and your Joan has only hared off in the ambulance with her!'

Fred's dark eyes glistened. 'Oh aye? Well good for her. It's a grand thing having a kid. You only ever think of yourself don't you? One day you'll end up a very lonely old woman Florence Oxby.'

She bristled. 'I'll not stop here to be insulted by the likes of you Fred Barratt!'

Turning on his heels, Fred stalked into the pub. A beer you didn't argue with.

On the Hoe, the Pagets sprawled wearily on rickety deckchairs, while a brass band played loudly behind them.

'What a racket,' moaned Len. 'Put a sock in it you lot!'

'Shut up you fool,' hissed his harassed wife. 'It's no wonder Lisa and Robert are always miserable with you grouching the way you do.'

Swearing under his breath, Len kicked out at a seagull threatening to steal his chips. 'Where are the kids anyway?' he queried angrily.

Vivien rose sharply from her seat. 'You were meant to be keeping an eye on them while I had a kip. For God's sake Len, jump to it. They could be anywhere!'

At exactly 4.30pm the midwife placed a tiny baby boy into the arms of an exhausted but ecstatic Sally.

'He's lovely, but I must say for a firstborn he was certainly in a hurry.'

Sally kissed her son's downy head. 'He was, wasn't he? Oh, the lady who came here with us, Joan Barratt, I think she's waiting outside. I know she'd love to see the baby.'

Feasting his eyes on his son, Brian nodded. 'Yes, Joan's been a brick.'

The midwife smiled. 'Well first we'll get you cleaned up, then you can go back on the ward, but only a short visit mind. You'll be needing your rest.'

Within the confines of the cosy terraced cottage, Rex Firkin drew reluctantly away from the voluptuous body of the lovely Pat and sighed. 'I'm afraid it's time to go love. Maybe I'll manage a weekend soon.'

His mistress patted his broad backside. 'Let's not count on it love.' Rising languidly, she glanced out at the busy scene on the Barbican. 'Oh Rex. Come here quick! Isn't this your wife?'

Rex swore as he gazed down at the grim-faced woman heading towards the cottage. The game was up, but just who could have told her?

Most of the passengers were making their way to the coach, but for the Pagets the last few hours had been a nightmare. The police were alerted by the frantic couple after a brief search for the children proved fruitless, and now, as they sat opposite a stony-faced officer in the city's Charles Cross police station, their spirits were at rock bottom.

'What on earth are we going to do?' anguished Vivien. 'They could well have been abducted!'

The officer was grim. 'Some people don't deserve to have kids. You should have kept your eyes on them constantly.' Shaking his head, he tutted.

'How dare you!' yelled Vivien. 'We love our kids. Do you think we willed them to disappear?'

Len gripped his overwrought wife's arm. 'Hush Viv. They are doing all they can.'

Suddenly a police officer popped his head around the door. 'Excuse me serge, but there's a Mr Fred Barratt at the desk and with him two children fitting the description of Lisa and Robert Paget. Says he found them wandering and recognised the pair as being on his coach this morning.'

There was a commotion as the family were reunited, and Len pumped Fred's hand warmly. However, the sergeant had the final say as the Pagets were about to depart. 'It's a happy ending for you and your kids, thanks to Mr Barratt here, but let it be a lesson to you. Now you'll have to look slippy if you're going to catch your coach.'

Joan hauled up the steps and flopped down beside Fred. 'What a time I've had. You'll never believe it love.'

He gestured to his sulking sister-in-law behind them. 'She made it her business to tell me what's been going on. Everything alright then?'

Joan nodded happily. 'A little boy. He's lovely. Reminded me of our David you know. So how was your day Fred?'

He glanced back at the subdued Pagets in the back seat. 'Rather eventful as it happens. I'll tell you when we're on our way. Hello I don't remember that woman sitting behind the driver, do you?'

Joan craned her neck. 'Who cares. I just want to get home now. It's been a long day.'

A SMALL STORY
Jean Paisley

Candyfloss clouds were the only interruption in the bright blue sky. Beneath them was the hustle and bustle of everyday life carrying on regardless. People always found a way of ignoring the bad things that were happening and sometimes the good things as well. The city was buzzing; it was a bank holiday. Practically everybody had the day off work. The children dragged their parents around the shops trying to squeeze extra gifts out of them, and the elderly took time to sit on park benches and let the breeze blow them down memory lane. It was a day when anything could happen and anything was possible.

Huge teacups and saucers twirled around on the open town square, their bright colours brightening up the grey cobblestones. Emma sat in a green cup, Andy sat in a blue one and Zoe sat in a pink one which was her favourite colour.

As Emma swung her heels backwards and forwards in her seat she felt hat she had hit something under it. She looked down and there cringing back away from the light was a tiny creature dressed in green. You could hardly see him against the green cup.

Emma thought that she was seeing things but, she still placed her denim backpack open upon the floor so that he might use it to escape if, he did in fact actually exist at all. She waved to her friends Andy and Zoe as the ride came to an end.

They all went off to Mcdonald's and had some hot chocolate and a burger. Emma left her bag slightly open so that anything inside could breathe. She thought that her bag was a little bit heavier than it had been earlier on but, she could not bear to look inside until she got onto the train to go home. The children had come into town from a village on the outskirts and they had to be back for supper at eight.

Walking down the narrow country lane they soon came to Zoe's cottage and said goodnight, then Andy jumped over his gate waving as he ran up a small winding path. Emma walked in through her back gate and was just in time to see her mother Linda making their supper. 'I will just play in the garden until supper is on the table,' said Emma.

She ran towards their greenhouse which was at the bottom of the garden at the end of a flat green lawn. Going inside she closed the door. There was a small round stool next to a wooden bench and Emma sat down upon it. Placing her bag on the bench she took out a few small items, one handkerchief, a small purse and snuggled up asleep in the bottom of her bag there was a tiny green man.

Emma ran back indoors, she had an old shoe box that she could make into a comfortable bed. A few clean white handkerchiefs with a sponge under them would make a better bed for the little man than her backpack. She still thought that it as all a bit of a dream but, she decided to follow it and see just what might happen.

The little man was still asleep when she gently picked him up, placed him in his new bed and pulled one of her cotton handkerchief over him. The cool evening air never got inside the greenhouse. She put the box under the bench way back out of sight on the floor in case he wanted to get up and walk around in the night. The place smelled of beautiful flowers. They were prize blooms grown by her father so, the little man would be safe as no one outside of the family was ever allowed inside of the greenhouse.

Next day Emma was up early before school, she wanted to take some food and water down to the little man. She took a top from off a bottle and filled it with milk. Then, she broke up some cornflakes and dropped them in. Next she made some tiny jam sandwiches.

The little man had climbed upon the bench and was sitting on the edge. Emma sat next to him on the stool and asked him who he was. He spoke with a tiny voice and Emma had to put her ear next to his face just to hear him at all. He was hiding in someone's bag when they got onto the roundabout and seeing that everything around him was so green he thought that he was back in the country and so he climbed out. Then, the person picked up their bag and left the roundabout and he had been trapped.

His name he said was Pukk and he came from an ancient race who spent a lot of time playing tricks on the giants (who of course were Emma's folk).

Emma said, 'Could you help Father to win the Best-in-Show award with his flowers?' and Pukk said, 'Yes.' So, they had a pact. Emma would look after the little man and he would use his powers for good things.

Father had some orchids. They were striking and of every colour that you could think of. The marquee was full and people had their names under their produce as the judges walked on by. They could not believe their eyes when they got to Emma's father's stand for in amongst his coloured blooms were some large black orchids. He won first prize and everyone said that they never knew anyone who could keep such a huge secret. Emma was overjoyed and brought the little man some of his favourite chocolate Terry's Orange.

Everything seemed to be going very well until Pukk could not help being Pukk and getting up to his old tricks. Emma had let him walk on the lawn for a while and the dog next door had chased him around a bit. Next day the dog had gone completely bald. Unfortunately it had been a prize poodle before this so the neighbours were irate and blamed it on the lawn, saying that it must be full of chemicals.

Emma knew that Pukk would have to be taken home. There were woods nearby where it was rumoured that strange things happened there so, after school one evening she placed Pukk in her bag and set off.

They came across a hollow half way up a tree and Pukk said, 'This is home.'
Emma promised to visit him and bring him some of his favourite treats now and then and he promised her that he would not play any more tricks on her family.

Later on Emma wrote a poem about Pukk back at school and it won her the first prize. It was for having such a good imagination.

AN AMICABLE ARRANGEMENT
Joyce Walker

Candyfloss clouds were the only interruption in the bright blue sky. Beneath them was the hustle and bustle of everyday life carrying on regardless. People always found a way of ignoring the bad things that were happening and sometimes the good things as well. The city was buzzing; it was a bank holiday. Practically everybody had the day off work. The children dragged their parents around the shops trying to squeeze extra gifts out of them, and the elderly took time to sit on park benches and let the breeze blow them down memory lane. It was a day when anything could happen and anything was possible.

Kevin Harland, self-confessed layabout, loped off to the local park to escape his mother's nagging.

Joan, too, was escaping, from an empty house and a husband who was always too busy to be at home with her and sat forlornly at the edge of the pond throwing bread to the ducks.

She was quite attractive in a well-to-do way and Kevin, always on the lookout for talent decided to stop and talk.

'Penny for your thoughts,' he said.

'You wouldn't want to hear them,' she replied, throwing a crust into the murky water. As she did so a shaft of sunlight caught the gold band on her finger.

Never the sort of person to beat around the bush, he preferred the direct approach, 'Husband left you, has he?'

'In a manner of speaking, he's gone to Liverpool on business.' Then she added, ruefully, 'He's always away on business.'

A piece of information that sounded good to Kevin.

'What sort of business? I mean, what does he enjoy so much that he can stay away from a lovely lady like you?'

'Imports and exports,' she replied, blushing at his compliment, 'and what makes you say I'm a lovely lady?' Looking at her reflection in the pond Joan saw nothing lovely at all.

'All ladies are lovely,' he remarked, 'especially ones on the right side of thirty who have nothing better to do with their time than be kind to our feathered friends.'

'And what do you do?' she asked.

'I'm an observer.'

'An observer of what?'

'Overfed ducks and lonely married ladies and I sometimes cure their loneliness, for a fee,' he grinned. Then he added, truthfully, 'Actually I'm between jobs at the moment.'

'Oh? And what do you do when you aren't between jobs?' she asked.

'As little as possible,' he replied. 'That's why I'm between jobs more than I'm in them.'

She laughed. 'And what's your fee for making lonely ladies happy?'

'Depends entirely on the lady. How about a smile and a cup of coffee in your kitchen for starters and you can buy or cook me dinner afterwards.'

'After what?' she asked with feigned puzzlement.

'After I give you a little of what you need to stop you from being lonely.'

Joan wanted nothing more than to talk that day, but Kevin knew the time would come when she would want more from him and when she did, he would be there to give it to her, for a fee, of course.

For six months they saw each other at every possible opportunity. There were breaks in the relationship, naturally, but as the affair was just a casual arrangement between the two of them, the separations didn't really matter and when they were together they would go to the theatre or cinema, sometimes a night-club and all at her expense. Occasionally, she would take him out shopping and buy him a new outfit. All in all, keeping Joan happy was a very rewarding experience.

Even an amicable arrangement like the one he and Joan shared couldn't last forever, however and theirs ended abruptly one February afternoon when his mother called him to the door because he had been visited by a man named Nigel Hutton.

'Mr Harland?'

He had never seen the man before and he didn't like what he saw. His large frame filled the doorway as he said, 'You've been seeing my wife.'

Kevin gave him the innocent look that had got him out of a thousand scrapes in the past.

'Oh, don't play the innocent with me, little boy. I know all about your bit of fun. My wife's name is Joan, but perhaps you have so many women you don't remember her.'

Kevin looked for an avenue of escape, only to find that there was none.

'You'd best come in,' he said nervously.

'I thought you should be among the first to know that she's pregnant and as the child can't possibly be mine and you're the only other man she's been seeing, I assume it must be yours.'

Kevin's voice, when he spoke came out somewhere between a squeak and a croak, 'What makes you so sure the baby isn't yours?'

'I had mumps rather late in life and you know what that can do to a man.' After a pause, he said, menacingly, 'The time has come to pay Mr Hartland.' He watched Kevin squirm and it was obviously giving him great pleasure.

'I can't afford to pay for anything,' he said, the squeak in his voice becoming more pronounced, 'I haven't got any money.'

'You misunderstand me, Mr Harland, neither my wife nor I want your money.' He reached into his breast pocket. Kevin, convinced the stranger had a gun ducked instinctively.

There was a dull thud, followed by a prolonged silence. Two pairs of eyes stared at the airline ticket on the table between them. One with relief, the other with disdain.

'Joan and I have a great deal to thank you for. You have given her the one thing in life that I couldn't.' Kevin picked up the ticket and examined it. It was a single to Amsterdam. 'We have a vacancy for a sales rep in our Dutch branch, it pays £18,000 a year and with it goes an apartment overlooking Amsterdam harbour. All you have to do is keep the customers happy. I'm prepared to throw in another £5,000 of my own, on condition that you never come back here, or try to contact my wife. If you do, what I'll be offering you will be something much less generous. So tell me Mr Harland, do we have a deal?'

The answer was always going to be yes.

'Good. You'll forgive me if I don't shake on it. You see, I have an aversion to snakes.' As he made to leave, he said, 'It's been a pleasure doing business with you.'

Kevin grinned at his good fortune and as the smile spread across his face he thought that £23,000 a year and a flat overlooking Amsterdam harbour might even make the job worth keeping.

As he went upstairs to look for his passport and tell his mother of his good fortune, he couldn't help wondering how many lonely, beclogged women were waiting to be made happy in Holland, for a fee, of course.

THE GUARDIAN ANGEL
Stephen Hullyer

Candyfloss clouds were the only interruption in the bright blue sky. Beneath them was the hustle and bustle of everyday life carrying on regardless. People always found a way of ignoring the bad things that were happening and sometimes the good things as well. The city was buzzing; it was a bank holiday. Practically everybody had the day off work. The children dragged their parents around the shops trying to squeeze extra gifts out of them, and the elderly took time to sit on park benches and let the breeze blow them down memory lane. It was a day when anything could happen and anything was possible.

Jane sat on the seat, beside her mother, Sue and contentedly licked her vanilla ice cream. They were both taking a well-earned rest from another frenzied afternoon's shopping.

As Jane lazily swung her legs backwards and forwards, she looked up. The ice cream dropped from her hand and ran down her T-shirt like an avalanche of snow. Standing just a short distance away was an alien, dressed in a sort of white space suit and he was looking right at her. Jane turned towards her mother. It was obvious from her lack of reaction that she couldn't see the alien.

At that same moment Sue turned and looked down at Jane. 'Oh, Jane,' she exclaimed angrily. 'Look what you've done. That was clean on today!'

Jane looked down and saw the ice cream running down her top like a swollen river. 'I'm sorry, Mum,' she said, her face reddening with embarrassment as Sue took out several paper towels and attempted to clean up the mess. 'But didn't you see that alien all dressed in white?'

'Whatever are you talking about, Jane?' retorted Sue sharply.

'Didn't you see him? He was right there.' Jane stared at the place where the alien had stood.

Seemingly oblivious of her mother's attempt to clean her, Jane jumped up onto the seat to get a better look.

'That does it, young lady,' Sue shouted, grabbing Jane by the arms and hauling her down like a main sail in a tremendous storm. 'Your shopping trip is over!'

'No, you don't understand,' Jane blurted out as tears sprung into her eyes. 'He was there!'

'I understand all too well,' Sue snapped, leading Jane away, with a vice-like grip on her arm. 'God knows what your father's going to say when he hears about this.'

'I thought we'd brought you up better than this,' Mark, Jane's father said. 'You should be old enough to own up to your mistakes and not to try and lie your way out of a situation.'

'But, Dad, I'm telling the truth,' Jane persisted. 'I did see someone. He was dressed in some sort of space suit.'

'Then maybe, you'd like to explain why no one else saw this strange figure, except you?'

Jane looked down at her feet dejectedly. 'I don't know but it *was* real. I didn't make it up and I'm sorry it made you angry.'

Mark hugged Jane affectionately. 'Don't you think you ought to tell your mother that?'

That night, after Jane had gone to bed, Mark and Sue talked about the day's events. 'Do you think she's coming down with something?' asked Sue anxiously.

'She doesn't appear to be,' replied Mark. 'Whatever she saw, it is as real as you and I.'

'What then? Puberty?'

'Let's forget it for now,' Mark said, reaching over and turning out the light.

Tuesday afternoons was games. For Jane this meant rounders. As she stood on the edge of the diamond, brandishing the rounders bat like it was a weapon, the white ball was lobbed towards her. Jane threw a tremendous swipe at it but missed. The momentum of the swing twirled her around and she fell to the round like a fairy fallen off her pedestal.

Jane quickly gathered her senses together and leapt again to her feet.

'Keep your eye on the ball, Jane,' yelled out Miss Simpson, the PE instructor.

The white ball was lobbed once more and again Jane missed it.

'This is your last time, Jane,' Miss Simpson said. 'Remember, don't take your eyes off the ball.'

The white ball, for the last time, was lobbed towards Jane. It seemed to climb slowly towards its zenith before descending rapidly like a rolling stone down a hill.

Jane's face was a mask of concentration before launching the bat forward. She heard and felt the healthy sound as the bat connected firmly with the ball. All sound seemed to cease as everyone watched the ball climb higher and higher into the sky.

Jane felt lighter than air as she began to run towards the first base. As she rounded the first base Jane stopped sharply like a car performing an emergency stop. Standing in the middle of the field was the alien in the white astronaut suit. Jane watched with a mixture of morbid horror and fascination as one of the fielders chased after the ball, which was heading straight for the alien. Jane opened her mouth to call out but no sound came out.

The girl had now reached the alien figure but, instead of bumping into him, she ran straight through him like he wasn't there. The fielder picked up the white ball and threw it back to the base. Despite the yelling of the other girls, Jane stood rooted to the spot. The ball landed heavily on Jane's head, knocking her immediately unconscious.

The doctor said there was no long-term damage but, to be on the safe side, he recommended that Jane should have the rest of the week off.

'What happened out there?' Sue asked Jane, as she stroked some hair away from the enormous bruise that was forming on her forehead. 'The other girls said you stopped running and began pointing at something.'

Jane's bottom lip began to tremble as she fought back the tears. 'I'm scared, Mum. I saw that alien thing again. What's wrong with me? What's he want with me?'

'Now, sssh,' Sue said, trying to keep the concern out of her voice. 'The doctor said you must have plenty of rest.'

Once Jane was asleep, Sue rang Mark at work. 'What did the doctor say?' Mark asked.

'He gave her a clean bill of health,' said Sue. 'Apart from the bump on her head, she's fine.'

'Do we know how she got hit?'

Sue paused before answering. 'She says she saw that alien again.' There was a heavy silence on the other end of the phone as what had been said was digested and understood. 'Mark are you still there?'

'Yeah, I'm still here,' Mark said with a weary sigh.

'What do you think? Is she making it all up?'

'I don't think so,' replied Sue, gazing up at the ceiling as if seeking spiritual advice. 'I believe her, she's scared and very frightened.'

'So, what do we do now?'

'Let's give it to the end of the week. The doctor has signed her off until then.'

The next day Jane felt well enough to venture downstairs and watch some TV. She put on her favourite DVD and sat down to watch it. Sue came in a few minutes later and sat down beside her. Soon, both of them were laughing out loud.

After a while the TV screen started to become all fuzzy and the picture faded away. Jane looked over at her mother, who was still laughing away. What was going on? She sank herself further down into the sofa as if seeking safety from whatever was going to happen.

Suddenly the screen cleared and she saw a picture of their town and the Market Square where she had first seen the alien. The view then changed to open fields with an ugly-looking factory where workers, dressed like the alien, stooped over what looked like a bomb.

The scene then returned to the market square and she saw people falling to the ground with horrible burns all over their bodies. Then a giant digital clock face appeared, showing tomorrow's date, with the time frozen on midday.

Then, as strangely as the whole scene started, the picture faded and returned once more to the DVD. That's when Jane screamed . . .

'It's all right, Jane,' said Sue gently. 'You're safe now. Just tell your father what you told me.'

As soon as Jane had calmed down Sue called Mark at work and asked if he would come home immediately.

'We were watching TV when the screen faded,' explained Jane, rubbing her red, tear-stained eyes and leaning against her mum's side for comfort. 'I knew something wasn't right as Mum was still laughing.'

'What did you see?' Mark asked.

'I saw our town, then the market square, and then the whole scene changed to some ugly factory in the middle of a field, where workers in the same white suits as the person I saw, were working on some kind of bomb.'

'A bomb?' Mark queried, leaning forward. 'Are you sure?'

Jane nodded her head slowly like a schoolgirl who had to admit to her teacher that she'd done wrong. Tears once more threatened to run down her pale cheeks. 'I'm positive and then I saw tomorrow's date.'

'Tomorrow's date? What's significant about that?'

The tears that Jane had fought so hard to banish, returned with a vengeance. 'At . . . midday . . .' she said, through large gulps of air, ' . . . people . . . will . . . start . . . to . . . die!' She finally gave in to her pain and cried herself to sleep beside her mother.

'What are we going to do?' Sue asked, for the hundredth time. She hated to sound like a worn out record but she didn't know what else to say.

'Something I should have done before,' Mark said, taking out his mobile phone and dialling a number.

'Who are you calling?'

'I'm calling my friend, Doug,' said Mark, covering the receiver with his hand. 'He's a journalist and he has his contacts. If anyone can find out the truth, he can.'

They had just finished breakfast when someone hammered on their front door furiously. Mark leap up from the table and was at the door within two strides.

'You could be onto something,' Doug said, taking out his notepad. As we all know this town was built in the early sixties. Before then it was just green fields until some kind of government building was built on it. Whatever building was there, it was highly top secret and I had to call in a couple of big favours.'

'Spare me the heroics,' Mark said brutally. 'Just tell me what you found. If I'm right you might have just landed the biggest story ever.'

Like any journalist, Doug knew when he'd landed a scoop. 'According to my sources, that place used to make nerve toxins.'

Mark eyes widened with amazement.

'So, what do you want to do now?' Doug asked, putting his notepad away.

Mark glanced quickly at his watch. 'We need to get over to the council offices, 'cause according to my watch, we have less than three hours to go.'

'So, let me get this straight,' said the council official, rising up from his chair and turning to look out the window. 'You expect me to bring this busy town to a standstill on some X-File type paranoia about an old government building, that may or may not have existed.

As Doug opened his mouth to say something the phone on the desk rang. The council official answered it and then looked up. 'What time did you say this tragedy was supposed to happen?'

Mark glanced at the clock on the wall. It read eleven-thirty. 'About midday,' he said simply. 'Why?'

'A policeman has just reported that ten pigeons fell out of the sky dead and some members of the public have reported feeling nauseous.'

'Where?' Mark asked, trying to keep the excitement out of his voice.

'The Market Square,' the official answered solemnly.

Pandemonium ensued as people were evacuated and the whole area was cordoned off. Members of the bomb disposal team went to work urgently. Mark glanced nervously at his watch. Half an hour to go before 'doomsday'.

Luckily, the bomb disposal team had just got to the bomb before it was too late. As they removed the bomb they found the remains of a skeleton underneath it. Various rumours circulated around as to how the skeleton got there and were never proved but Jane always believed that the strange figure she saw was the ghost of the dead scientist.

THE ROSES OF PICCARDY
Chris Senior

Candyfloss clouds were the only interruption in the bright blue sky. Beneath them was the hustle and bustle of everyday life carrying on regardless. People always found a way of ignoring the bad things that were happening and sometimes the good things as well. The city was buzzing; it was a bank holiday. Practically everybody had the day off work. The children dragged their parents around the shops trying to squeeze extra gifts out of them, and the elderly took time to sit on park benches and let the breeze blow them down memory lane. It was a day when anything could happen and anything was possible.

But it was the door Alice noticed above all else. Apart from the door, the garden itself remained unchanged. A sturdy box privet enclosed beds of Sweet Williams and riotous orange and yellow marigolds on three sides. Lilac trees, lavender bushes and rhododendrons jostled with exotic and immaculate camellias and neat rows of blush roses that bloomed in profusion like sun warmed pot-pourri in crumpled velvet sachets. Alice closed her eyes in contentment. She had always loved the roses best of all.

The door was set in the old stone wall that protected the delicate roses from the wind and formed the fourth side of the garden's perimeter. It was almost hidden by a riot of honeysuckle that spilled over the worn stones like a perfumed waterfall. It was the strangest door that Alice had ever seen. It appeared to be opening and shutting itself and chuckling with laughter. 'Come in. Come in,' invited the door.

As it chuckled open Alice found herself standing at the beginning of a long passage. 'Welcome, welcome,' laughed the door as it closed itself firmly behind her. As Alice stepped forward the door slowly drifted away leaving her standing in a long glass corridor. Huge crystals hung from its high ceiling almost touching the floor in places. They shimmered and glinted with a cool blue light that Alice found restful and soothing. From the shadowy depths of the glass wall Alice could now see row upon row of carved faces.

'They look almost alive,' Alice whispered to herself.

'That's because we are,' echoed a chorus of gentle voices. 'We are the faces of yesterday, today and tomorrow. We can see the past, the present and the future. Our eyes have seen everything there is to see in the world and everything that is yet to be seen. Our ears have heard everything that has ever been said and every word yet to be spoken. Pass on your way and remember.'

'Remember what?' asked Alice.

'All that has been said and all that there is still left to say,' chorused the voices.

Alice was silent for a moment. But that doesn't make sense she thought. How can I remember things that haven't been said yet.

'No one said it would make sense,' whispered the voices as the faces gradually faded away. Alice stood for a while watching her own face staring back at her and then began the long walk down the corridor.

As her eyes became more accustomed to the dim light Alice noticed a circle of light which grew bigger and brighter the closer she got to it. To her delight the circle turned out to be two giant crystals that fitted neatly into smooth hollows in the ceiling and the floor. Alice saw that the crystals were turning slowly and felt herself being drawn into the brilliant shower of light.

'Welcome to the doorway of destiny,' said a smiling voice. A tall silver-haired man glided noiselessly towards her out of the brilliance.

'Please pass on your way and remember.'

As Alice stepped towards the revolving light, the corridor disappeared and she found herself on a busy esplanade. An important looking head waiter approached her and placed a tray in her hands.

'Daydreaming again. Always daydreaming,' he muttered distractedly.

'Take this down to table twenty-four and be quick about it.'

Alice looked around. Where was table twenty-four she wondered. She began to walk slowly along the esplanade deftly avoiding the crush of people all intent on seeing and being seen. After walking for some time Alice found herself at the top of a flight of steps. Smoothed to a shine by countless feet, the steps wound steeply down parallel to the sea wall. About halfway down the steps ended at a narrow stopping place, then meandered about even more steeply until they reached a shingle beach far below. Turning to ask somebody if this was the right place Alice saw the head waiter waddling up and down in a fussy manner that was most unbecoming. She stared at his back as he disappeared into the crowd.

'He looks for all the world like a pompous penguin,' Alice giggled to herself.

In a sudden flurry of activity a group of chattering people pushed past her and began to climb down the steps.

'Hey waitress. You there.' A portly gentleman in a shiny waistcoat and yellow spats came towards Alice. His large cigar dropped ash over the tea tray as he leant over the sea wall and looked at the beach below. 'Afternoon tea by jove. Just what the doctor ordered. A fellow works up quite an appetite romancing the ladies don't you know.' He winked at Alice and blew a large smoke ring into the air. 'Come on then my girl. Doesn't do to keep the ladies waiting.'

Alice adjusted her white frilly cap and apron. Carefully balanced the loaded tray on her upturned hand and began the slow descent to the beach. The tray was lavishly full. As well as chocolate eclairs and crumpets with honey there was a pot of lemon tea. Silver cutlery. A china tea service patterned with roses. Long stemmed crystal glasses. Wafer thin cucumber sandwiches. Strawberries and cream and a bottle of chilled champagne.

Alice felt herself floating effortlessly down the worn steps as though the tray was weightless. She giggled to herself again. What ever would Flo and Edna back in the nursing home say if they could see her now? The crippling arthritis that had confined her to a wheelchair and bent and gnarled her once nimble fingers had miraculously vanished and Alice felt young and free again. Unable to make head or tail of what was happening Alice stopped thinking about it and decided to enjoy her new found vitality to the full.

The portly gentleman had somehow got down to the beach already and waved at her. Alice deftly placed the tray onto his picnic table. The ladies seated under the bright umbrella continued their conversation. Alice smiled to herself. She had been a waitress during the First World War when she met Mitch. He had been so handsome in his officer's uniform. All the girls were mad for him but it was Alice he courted and married.

Turning back to the steps Alice realised with amazement and irritation that they were no longer there. Way above her head on the crowded esplanade Alice could see the fussy head waiter. He was leaning over the rail waving vigorously. Alice thought he looked more like a penguin than ever.

'Silly man,' Alice murmured to herself as she began to look for another way up. 'If he's not careful he'll take a nasty tumble and spoil his smart suit.'

Noticing a crowd of people further along the beach Alice hurried towards them. In front of the eager crowd Alice saw a large wooden stage with a backdrop depicting a battle scene. Children in their Sunday best clothes ran about in the warm sunshine rolling hoops and calling excitedly to each other. The rising buzz of conversation quietened as a roll of drums announced the start of the show. Alice smoothed her hair and tipped her straw sun bonnet forward a little to shield her eyes from the glare of the sun.

The crowd waited expectantly as the stage filled up with life-sized toy soldiers. They stood to attention in their crimson tunics their faces impassive behind waxed moustaches and bushy side whiskers. Alice held her breath. The crowd began to murmur amongst themselves as the silence became oppressive. Suddenly with a clash of cymbals the stage was bathed in a brilliant light. The soldiers levelled their guns and began to fire into the crowd swollen now by a sea of khaki uniforms. A chorus line of high kicking girls in spangled tights appeared. Dancing a complicated routine through the bursts of gunfire they scattered red petals over the fallen men and the cheering children waving flags. The firing ceased as suddenly as it had begun. The drummer boy beat out a retreat. The stage darkened and emptied. Subdued mothers called to their children and hurried them away. Alice looked back to see more people rushing down the beach towards the stage as a marching band warmed up the crowd for the second performance.

Alice walked along the beach lost in thought. Rusty broken rifles and battered tin helmets littered the sand. Several times Alice had to avoid rolls of barbed wire and discarded gas masks that stretched across her path. Exhausted she stopped and sat down on a large stone that had originally formed part of the coastal defences.

Mitch had been killed on the Somme. Her handsome young husband so loving and dear had been lost to her forever. At first Alice had wanted her own life to end, and although her broken heart had eventually healed, the scars had remained. She had continued to love Mitch for the rest of her life and had never remarried. There had been lovers of course and other offers of marriage, but somehow it didn't seem right to accept what she thought of as second best. Alice thought despite her loss she had lived a long and a full life. Her one regret was that she had never had children but she had nephews, nieces and godchildren to love and her voluntary work kept her occupied. So on the whole she was content. Even the crippling arthritis had failed to dampen her enthusiasm for getting the most out of life. Alice shivered. Lost in her thoughts she suddenly became aware of the cool sea breeze and the darkening sky.

A ribbon of twinkling lights suddenly snapped on along the esplanade as the evening crowds made their way excitedly towards the funfair. As Alice ran lightly up from the beach she could hear her favourite tune playing on the steam carousel.

'Roses are shining in Piccardy in the hush of the evening dew. Roses are flowering in Piccardy but there's never a rose like you.'

As Alice stood in wonder a full baritone voice took up the song. 'And though roses may die in the summertime and although we are so far apart. There is one rose that blooms not in Piccardy. That's the rose that I keep in my heart.'

Mitch was waiting for her smiling his familiar loving smile. His moustache and side whiskers were neatly trimmed above his starched collar. His blue eyes were sparkling.

Placing his arm around her waist Mitch swung Alice light as a feather onto a golden prancing horse and with a grin clambered up behind her.

'I've been waiting for you for ages,' he whispered in Alice's ear. 'I thought you were never coming.' Falling and rising; the horses began their stately ride. As the steam engine powered the huge carousel, Alice leant back into Mitch's strong arms and smiled.

LIFE'S SURPRISES
David Bruce Moffatt

Candyfloss clouds were the only interruption in the bright blue sky. Beneath them was the hustle and bustle of everyday life carrying on regardless. People always found a way of ignoring the bad things that were happening and sometimes the good things as well. The city was buzzing; it was a bank holiday. Practically everybody had the day off work. The children dragged their parents around the shops trying to squeeze extra gifts out of them, and the elderly took time to sit on park benches and let the breeze blow them down memory lane. It was a day when anything could happen and anything was possible.

It was then that we suggested that we take the children away for the weekend as they had been pestering their parents for toys in the shops. We could not get into a decent hotel at this last minute, so we had booked into this cheap guest house on recommendation. It was clean and the food was good.

We were sitting on the seafront bench on this not-too-warm a day, the clouds changing from candyfloss to that black look coming over the horizon. As it was a bank holiday, we had hoped for a blue sky. The seaside is lovely when the sun is shining, but the black clouds turn it into hell, as you know you are a long way from home with only the landlady in the guest house to return to. Quite amiable when the sun shines, as she knows you will be out all day on the beach with your grandchildren. She could take it easy for she needed no entertainment. Bank holidays are their busy time, they are fully booked. Children all screaming indoors, when it is wet: it is not their kind of bank holiday, but England being as it is, it was all you could expect. The wind had come up as well and the newspapers, which people had been reading and dropped, had started to blow about. Their readers chasing them, arguing whose was whose and the children getting most of the flack. Storm clouds from all directions, I thought. I was glad that my children had grown up and I had not the worry of entertaining them.

The wind seemed to drop as quickly as it had started and the sun came again. The black clouds disappeared, back to enjoying the beach and the landlady breathed a sigh of relief. No lines full of clothes, only the towels and swimming costumes.

It was a sudden bang which startled us. It came from a small boat with an outboard with their clothes looking as though on fire. People rushed down to the sea's edge not realising that they could do nothing. The lifeboat maroon went off and rockets blew into the air. The lifeboat rushed out. It seemed to come from nowhere. Children all shouting with excitement, we just sat still and watched hoping that no one had been hurt. The boat was still burning as the lifeboat pulled alongside, spraying foam from its jets and putting out the fire in no time. The passengers of the little boat were climbing aboard the lifeboat and we could see they were all wearing their red lifejackets and were not on fire.

On this bank holiday we did have some excitement, something for the children to tell their parents and their friends back at school. No one had sustained any injury, it had been a gas cylinder which had exploded when some young people had been having a picnic with a primus stove.

Bank holidays do have their ups and downs and good times as well. We did record it on the camcorder. Our trip to the seaside to Brixham in South Devon had turned into something quite different from that which we had expected.

It was on the way home that we realised we had left one of our suitcases behind. Had it been full of our clothes, it would not have mattered so much, but it was full of the presents which the children had bought for their parents. They were most upset so we turned round to collect them. When turning the corner the landlady came running out shouting:

'Fire. It's the chip pan,' not expecting to see us. 'More trouble for you?' she asked.

'No, we left our presents behind.'

'I know, I have sent them on by post for I did not expect you to return so quickly.'

The fire engine arrived and ran out the hoses. We just turned and left. We were not needed as the landlady said:

'Bank holidays are my nightmares.'

We did return the following year and found the very smart, newly painted kitchen. The bench by the sea, just the same. The weather marvellous and no more interruptions. The grandchildren were away on a foreign holiday with their parents, their treat this time.

HAVE A NICE DAY
Barbara Grossman

*Candyfloss clouds were the only interruption in the bright blue sky.
Beneath them was the hustle and bustle of everyday life carrying on
regardless. People always found a way of ignoring the bad things that
were happening and sometimes the good things as well. The city was
buzzing; it was a bank holiday. Practically everybody had the day off
work. The children dragged their parents around the shops trying to
squeeze extra gifts out of them, and the elderly took time to sit on park
benches and let the breeze blow them down memory lane. It was a day
when anything could happen and anything was possible.*

'Would you like me to hold the tray?'

Lauren turned towards the voice. Against the morning sunshine,
generously streaming through the windows of the motorway cafeteria, a
tall slightly built girl stood, arms outstretched in anticipation. Lauren
handed her the tray containing a cup of coffee and plate of biscuits.

'Thanks, you're a godsend.' Now she was free to hold Katy with
both arms.

The girl followed her to a table, waited as Lauren sat down, then
placed the tray on the table. Again Lauren thanked her. She shuffled her
feet self-consciously. 'That's OK.'

Inviting her to sit down, Lauren held the plate out to the girl. 'Have
a biscuit!' It was demurely declined. The girl was thin, too thin, as if
she hadn't eaten for some time. 'Perhaps you'd prefer a sandwich?'
Lauren asked coaxingly.

'I'm not hungry, thanks all the same.'

The girl's refusal was decisive, almost as if she resented the
benevolent gesture. Lauren shrugged her shoulders, a little peeved at the
rejection.

Drinking her coffee slowly, Lauren studied the girl. About 18 years
old, most probably a student, they all seemed to wear the same gear;
blue jeans with loose fitting top. A quiet girl not much emotion. Now
and then she furtively looked around the crowded tables, then lowered
her head. Lauren interpreted her behaviour as shyness.

'Are you going far?' The girl's enquiry broke her train of thoughts.

'We're going to Oxford,' Lauren playfully tickled Katy under the
chin.

'Going to stay with Nanna and Grandpa for a few days, aren't we sweetie?'

Lauren smilingly looked at the girl. She quickly averted her eyes.

'Perhaps the baby talk embarrassed her.'

'Where are you going?' Lauren asked with interest. There was a moment of hesitation before the girl replied. 'Just past Oxford.'

Lauren smiled in surprise. 'That is a coincidence. Have you driven far?'

The girl shifted nervously. 'I . . . I haven't got a car, I've been thumbing lifts.'

'Poor thing,' Lauren felt an empathy, remembering her own hard-up student days. 'Would you care for a lift as far as Oxford?'

The girl's face lit up, becoming animated for the first time. 'Great that'll be fine.'

Lauren rose. 'Wait here, I'll just pop into the 'ladies' and see to baby.' She turned back to the girl. 'What's your name?'

The girl didn't answer immediately, then quietly said, 'Debbie.'

'Well Debbie, I'm Lauren and this little bundle is Katy.'

The girl nodded, then anxiously asked, 'You won't be long, will you?'

Cheeky, Lauren thought, still, she was pleased to have some company on the journey.

Surprisingly, the girl asked to sit at the back of the car with the carrycot and Katy. During the journey she was reticent, only speaking in reply to Lauren's questions, and even then guardedly. To ease the atmosphere Lauren switched on the radio. 'Just in time for the news Debbie.'

'Turn it off!' The girl's voice was loud and menacing. Realising she had startled Lauren, she lowered her voice. 'Sorry, I've a bit of a headache.' She put her hands up to her head. Concerned, Lauren asked if she would like an aspirin.

'No!' The girl quickly assured her. 'I'll be alright.'

In the mirror, Lauren could see the girl's face, ashen, her dark eyes staring. There was something about her eyes - Lauren shivered slightly. Now she regretted giving the girl a lift. She would stop at the next service station for petrol, then somehow make a plausible excuse to get rid of her.

'I'm going to pull into that garage,' Lauren made her voice sound light-hearted. The girl leaned forward, one hand gripping the carrycot.

'No, you're not!' she hissed. 'You'll keep on driving until I tell you to stop!'

Lauren's hands clutched the wheel trying to control her mounting panic, keeping her voice steady. 'And if I don't?'

The girl smiled sardonically. 'You wouldn't want anything to happen to your precious baby - would you?' She prodded Lauren's back.

Lauren felt sick. 'I'll drive anywhere you say, please don't hurt my baby,' Lauren pleaded, her mind numb with horror. Fear for Katy rose, almost choking her. She had made the cardinal error of giving a stranger a lift, something she had vowed never to do. The girl had seemed harmless and innocent, yet little peculiarities were there. She should have detected the warning signals. Through her stupid lapse, her baby was now in danger.

If only she could turn the clock back to early morning. Fixing her mind on the sanity of those hours, when David had kissed Katy and herself before leaving for the airport. She had held Katy in her arms and waved goodbye. David's last words were, 'Have a nice day.' The journey had begun with such happiness, looking forward to spending a few days with her parents. Katy was their pride and joy, their only grandchild.

'Don't drive so fast!' The girl's shrill penetrating voice broke through Lauren's yearning thoughts, bringing her back to the desperate reality. The safety of Katy was paramount. I mustn't do anything to antagonise her. Should I try reasoning with her? Looking at the girl's frenzied eyes, Lauren knew it would he hopeless.

The girl ordered her to take routes which ended up on roads with which Lauren was not familiar. A police car cruised by, its occupants glancing at them. Anticipating Lauren's thoughts, the girl whispered threateningly. 'If they stop, I'll get the baby before they get me.'

'Why are you doing this?' Lauren hoarsely implored.

The girl looked blankly at her. To Lauren's relief her rage seemed to have subsided, she had loosened her grip on the carrycot. How long would that last? Her anguished thoughts were answered.

The girl began to breathe heavily, then venomously spat out, 'I hate babies!'

'Why?' Lauren whispered.

The girl stared through Lauren then began to ramble. 'It's alright for them, they can't do anything wrong.'

Lauren asked softly, 'Who?'

The girl grimaced. 'The twins, I hate them!' Her face was distorted with hate. 'She should have stayed with my dad, not that man, they're not my sisters, I hate them!' She continued the tirade which was now incoherent; but Lauren had heard enough to understand what had happened. Exhausted from her rantings, the girl lay back against the seat, her body making convulsive movements. Gradually she became still. Lauren prayed she would stay that way. She must think of something to do without causing suspicion.

The petrol gauge showed there was just enough for a couple of miles. Driving for ages, she didn't know where she was. Katy began to fret. Lauren's blood froze. Her crying might trigger the girl off into action. She was approaching a garage. 'I must get some petrol,' Lauren urgently informed the girl. Grudgingly she agreed.

'I'll keep the baby with me, and my eyes on you the whole time.'

'No!' Lauren shook her head. 'I'm not leaving my baby.'

The girl smiled crookedly. 'Please yourself. If you don't do or say anything, she'll be alright.'

Lauren filled up with petrol then went into the shop. It was empty, except for a young male assistant behind the till. She asked him for a pen, praying that the girl would think she was paying by credit card. Finding a scrap of paper in her bag, she began writing a message for help. The door burst open, the girl stood in the doorway clutching Katy. 'Hurry up Lauren, the baby is getting restless.' She smiled sweetly to the assistant. He smiled back. Lauren closed her eyes, she felt faint. All seemed so natural to the boy, how could he suspect that the girl was insane. Her last chance had gone. She swayed.

'You alright?' The boy looked concerned.

'She's alright don't worry,' the girl turned to Lauren and said mockingly. 'I told you not to eat that burger.'

The boy laughed. 'Those burgers can give you indigestion.'

Lauren forced her lips into a smile and paid the bill. She felt weak and vulnerable, there was no hope.

The girl led the way back to the car, half running. Lauren saw a police car driving towards the exit. Her mouth dried. What if the girl had seen it. No, she was too intent on getting into the car. Waiting until the girl had placed Katy into the carrycot, Lauren drove towards the exit, passing the police car. She drove very slowly, not to attract their attention.

'Oh God!' They were flashing their lights and beckoning her to pull over. Terror took hold of her as the girl shouted hysterically.

'You bitch, what have you done?'

'Nothing, I swear nothing,' Lauren sobbed. She stopped the car, the police officers were approaching. It was now or never. Summing up all her physical and mental strength, with one swift movement, Lauren twisted herself round and over the back of the seat, falling on top of the surprised girl, at the same time screaming for help. She felt a sharp burning sensation in her arm, then the police had the girl out of the car struggling and screaming.

Making sure Katy was alright, Lauren got out of the car. The girl, now overpowered, was shrieking obscenities at Lauren. A policewoman arrived and took the girl away.

The officer helped Lauren into the back of the police car, she sank down on the seat. Her arm was hurting. She touched it, it was wet and sticky. The officer bent down and gently examined it. 'You've a slight knife wound, nothing serious,' then jocularly added, 'you'll live, we'll soon get you to hospital.'

Lauren stared at him, 'She had a knife?'

'Yes, she must have taken it from the cafeteria. We traced her that far.' He patted Lauren's shoulder lightly. 'You and the baby are very lucky she didn't use it.'

The carrycot with Katy in was brought into the police station. Though her arm was painfully hurting her, Lauren picked up Katy and hugged her. Thank God she was safe.

During the drive to the hospital, Lauren learned that the girl had absconded from a mental institution, having attempted to harm her stepsisters. Lauren shivered at what might have been if the police hadn't stopped her. Yet, in spite of the state of terror and anguish the girl had inflicted on her, she felt a twinge of compassion. The girl was someone's child, the mother must be devastated. It was then she suddenly remembered her parents. They must be distraught at her non-arrival. The officers promised they would contact them as soon as they reached the hospital.

The sun was just setting as they drew up. The deep red sky signalled the end of the day. It must have been a wonderful bank holiday weather-wise, but, Lauren reflected, not for her. It would certainly be one she'd never forget.

Before Lauren got out of the car, there was something she had to know. Her voice weak with fatigue she asked. 'Why did you stop me?'

One of the officers turned round and reprovingly answered, 'You weren't wearing your seat belt.'

Lauren sobbed and laughed with relief. Her first error had almost cost her baby's life, the second one had saved it.

HOLIDAY MEMORIES
Maurice Hope

Candyfloss clouds were the only interruption in the bright blue sky. Beneath them was the hustle and bustle of everyday life carrying on regardless. People always found a way of ignoring the bad things that were happening and sometimes the good things as well. The city was buzzing; it was a bank holiday. Practically everybody had the day off work. The children dragged their parents around the shops trying to squeeze extra gifts out of them, and the elderly took time to sit on park benches and let the breeze blow them down memory lane. It was a day when anything could happen and anything was possible.

Hi there! My name is Bobby Clark. Bobby Jnr, aged ten when these events that I'm going to tell you about what took place some 40 years ago. Days that will forever stay with me and my older sister Lucy. My telling of which was fuelled on hearing Kirsty McColl on the radio the other day telling us that guy down at the chip shop swears he's Elvis.

It was the day that the circus came to town. I was only ten at the time and my sister, Lucy, my bossy sister Lucy, was 13. Her friend, Sally Beth Kennedy had come with us. To both, supposedly, help look after me and because her folks could never afford the time to be away from their dairy farm across the river from us a few miles outside of Greenboro. It was a pretty spot, down in the fertile bottomland, a good farm. Sally Beth's mother, father and elder brother, Jake who was barely 17 had to work hard, damn hard to make ends meet. But things had improved during the last few years. Every once in a while either Jake or her would get to go to town with their mom. The Kennedys, just like we were, they too were a real close family.

When my father and mother moved out to Stockton Forge, the farm next but one to them, it was for us all about the best thing that could happen to us. I can still remember the happy smile on Sally Beth's face the night we all sat outside and talked, played music and the older folks, drank moonshine whisky. It sparkled. Oh boy, her smile captured my heart. When I looked at her, which I did a whole lot, my heart thumped against my chest and all of a sudden I found myself swallowing hard. I had fallen in love.

Like I mentioned a little earlier, we were at the circus. A mite small compared to some circus acts today, but us kids just loved the excitement, the dreams of running away with them and there were the rides, the carnival that was parked up in the park alongside of it. Our minds bedazzled by the smiles of the clowns, female riders, slipping on and off the finely groomed Palomino ponies and the trapeze acts launching themselves through the air later that evening. What, with us eating the popcorn and shoving our faces into the pink candyfloss - between our shrill cries of joy, the chill of the night air was never felt by any of us kids.

As we watched the exhilarating shows we were entertained by the likes of freaks of nature, a horse, a donkey and a pet monkey that climbed the tent pole and threw peanuts at us. It was a great night. Mom, dressed in her new Levis and a pink summer top and yellow headscarf - she looked like a movie star. Marilyn Monroe I thought must have looked a lot like Mom, her blonde hair an' all. Dad, he would keep sneaking off from us kids, get himself a drink and try his hand at gambling and meet up with some friends from the valley.

While we loved the day, it never quite gained the attention of our tales of reflection like when, a couple of years earlier - Dad, Mom, Lucy and myself went down to a state fair in Louisiana where Elvis Presley was playing. There he was, this lanky, near skinny guy with his swinging guitar, wooing the girls - either when he got to play on the main stage later in the evening or playing from the back on an open flat-bottom truck. The crowds of young people clamouring to get near to him. From that day on he became Lucy's biggest idol.

Oh, I treasured that day, loving the way that Elvis sang and the music played. Tucked to his left and back a couple of steps behind Elvis was Scotty Moore, and boy couldn't he play that guitar. For days if not weeks I would play air-guitar as I listened to Elvis' 45 record of Heartbreak Hotel. Lucy and her friends swooned over the handsome, tanned features of Elvis. She had a picture tacked behind her bedroom door, another above her bed and a photo cut from a magazine mounted in a silver picture frame. She was plumb crazy about him, as were hundreds of other young and not so young girls. Myself, I was more into the music of Jerry Lee Lewis, Carl Perkins - the Sun sound, and the sibling harmonies of the Everly Brothers, Don and Phil, and as I grew older the Beatles, Rolling Stones and today, it is the Texas singer-songwriter crowd. Guy Clark, Rodney Crowell, Terry Allen, Robert

Earl Keen, Steve Earle and the late Townes Van Zandt plus the likes of Iris DeMent and Gillian Welch and her partner, Dave Rawlings.

Things have changed, today - not necessarily for the better, either. No longer do you have the Saturday picture shows or can one sample the same thrill of travelling down the likes of Route 66. Its truck stops, road houses and gas stations have nearly all gone since the new highways were opened, resulting in a whole culture being taken from us.

Going back to the day at the fair, all had gone great till the skies darkened and within minutes the thunder, it roared. Lightning lighting up the dark, blackened sky. Like a good few more we weren't sure what to do. On hindsight leave as fast as our legs could carry us would have been the best option. Dad, he wasn't for that nor was he particularly keen on staying once the rain came, but he did. Long enough to sample one of the heaviest deluges the country has ever experienced, within minutes the field was swimming in water. Streams of brown coloured water were running out through the circus tent.

It was then that the Palomino stallion dashed forth, trailing its reins. A frightened young boy was somehow hanging onto its neck. No saddle was on its back, but that wasn't to stop my dad as he threw himself at the rope. Catching it. In one movement he was spun, not once but twice and dragged along. Splashing through the water till the startled, half-crazy, half-scared pony steadied as it approached the opening in the fence that served as the gateway for the circus trucks and combine harvesters when the field was sown with wheat.

It was then that Dad regained his footing and, in one movement launched himself onto the back of the pony. Within seconds he had not only made it onto its back, but with the boy tucked against his left shoulder pulled up the pony to little more than a walk. Mom, Lucy and myself made our way towards him. Soaked as we were to the skin, we cared little that the rain was still coming down, steadily. Looking over at those parked up over by the gate, I could see our Studebaker parked between an open bed truck and Uncle Joe's powder blue Chevy.

Dad had saved the day, just as he did when there was a wreck out on Highway 64 when we were heading home after a family reunion down in Memphis with some cousins that I got to like later in life, though not just then. Lucy, she never did particularly like them, either. Why this was I could never really figure out, only that they were city folk and we were of farming stock. We found it hard getting to find some common ground with them other than they too had a mother and father.

Everything that we thought as being new they thought was old hat. They had either seen or heard it all before, but when it came to countrylife they were found to be more wanting than an alien. The one time that they came to the farm they couldn't throw a fishing line or had any idea of how to shoot a rifle. But, they hadn't a clue or knew how to throw a curve ball either. They were we thought, plain weird.

On coming on the wreck, Dad raced full charge to the overturned car - reaching in and in an instant got hold of a young man bleeding from a cut on his face and dragged him a full 60 yards into the field. It then became blurred, as first an orange fireball leapt forth and exploded. Dad was down, and he wasn't moving. Our hearts were pumping frantically, fear of frightening proportions had us held in a trance. Mom was first to move and boy, didn't she go. Falling on her knees she lent down, shouting at him to move as she shook him like a bag of beans. He still wasn't moving, then moving like a snake when it strikes, he spun Mom off her feet. Her arms swinging, tears of joy were running down her face as she was caught between striking him with her fists and clasping her hands round his neck as he pulled her close.

It wasn't till afterwards that the full impact of what he had done, placing his own life in immediate danger to save a young guy who had been visiting some old school friends out at Cross Ridge Junction. It never made the papers, but to us he was the greatest hero there ever was.

Going back to the Elvis show, it was a crazy time. Lucy and her friend got to the front of the screaming crowd where girls were fainting as he gyrated, thrust his guitar way up high and between songs - he would smile, mumble a few words as he flicked his fingers through his black, greasy hair. Girls went wild, and when he bent down to touch the outstretched arms the noise was deafening. One time his hand touched Sally Beth's and she all but crumpled in a heap. Such was the power and adulation generated by his presence. It was said by her brothers that she would not wash her upper arm for a week, nor let anyone touch the place.

Years later we all met up and spoke of that day. Sally Beth by which time had married, and had two kids of her own and was divorced. Lucy meanwhile, she was happily married and had two grown-up children or so they thought and were forever having to remind a protective Lucy. Though in reality they were just young college kids struggling to find themselves. Roy, her eldest he was set making a career in law, while his younger brother by just over a year, Danny he had illusions of becoming a full-time musician.

He had already won a bunch of championships in Kentucky. Though mainly for fiddle, he had also won a couple on mandolin and one for flat-picking guitar. He also got to make a number of appearances at festivals, both in a band and solo. Lucy, till now she had conveniently forgot about going to see Elvis and her brief sojourn in the music business. Only when I had left the room and the girls had the place to themselves did she open up. Telling of how for six months she held a recording contract with Columbia, had two singles and then vanished from sight. Her silliness that night seeing Elvis still makes her blush, for not only was Sally Beth's arm touched by his, but she left him her telephone number for him to call the next time that he was in town, and he did. Many times. Albeit being all in her sweetest dreams, she forever held those happy thoughts close to her ever loving heart. Silly, sure it was, but what would life be without some silliness?

STREET EVANGELIST
Carolyn Davidson

Candyfloss clouds were the only interruption in the bright blue sky. Beneath them was the hustle and bustle of everyday life carrying on regardless. People always found a way of ignoring the bad things that were happening and sometimes the good things as well. The city was buzzing; it was a bank holiday. Practically everybody had the day off work. The children dragged their parents around the shops trying to squeeze extra gifts out of them, and the elderly took time to sit on park benches and let the breeze blow them down memory lane. It was a day when anything could happen and anything was possible.

Amidst the hubbub of the busy High Street, a place I knew only too well, I stood alone surveying the scene. The city centre was much the same as it had always looked on a busy morning; full of shoppers and passers-by too busy to stop and notice me. As I scanned the street I noticed the many faces; different people from diverse walks of life; different ages, ethnic backgrounds; a business man in a smart suit, holidaymakers with cameras and bored locals. It was not Carnival Week or Racing Day, yet there was a sense of expectancy in the air. I sensed that all these people had been gathered together in this place for a particular reason, a special event, about which they knew nothing. The significance of the moment perceived, perhaps, only by my spirit, seemed to have eluded them completely. They continued walking aimlessly.

Then suddenly, as I observed the scene, the sky darkened, clouds gathered overhead as though a violent thunderstorm were approaching, yet still there was no rain or lightning. A low rumble filled the air, like the sound of an underground train. A few yards away from where I stood, the ground suddenly split open. Fire burst from the chasm. What followed is hard to describe . . . the chaos and panic of the crowd, the desperation and fear of people who had, a few moments ago, been walking around leisurely. Some began rushing about, clutching their throats and chests, some, suffering heart attacks, dropped to the ground.

I knew that what was happening was yet another of the signs foretold by John the Evangelist, prophesied 2000 years ago. Bible open in hand, I ran from person to person, trying desperately to explain what was happening and how to escape the coming wrath, but no one wanted to listen; some pushed me away, some just ran, trying, in vain, to avoid whatever it was they believed was coming. I saw the man in the smart suit run by, desperately clawing at his necktie, gasping for air, as his heart failed him.

Age-old trees, which had sheltered countless generations from the summer heat, were uprooted like small weeds by the shuddering ground; iron railings buckled like molten wax and sank into the earth. The pavement beneath our feet moved like a giant conveyor belt and then rippled like linen billowing on the washing line on a windy day. All around people died of fear; corpses littered the walkways; buildings and rows of shops collapsed like walls of cards, their glass window fronts shattering. Timber and metal, scrunched up like paper, were littered everywhere. Somehow I knew that what was occurring now was not just local but world-wide. Among the devastation I praised God, knowing that the prophecy was coming to pass in my own lifetime, before my very eyes. The scene was awesome and I was struck with wonder. Suddenly, it was as though a rug had been pulled form under my feet; everything began sliding, slipping, breaking . . . then I woke up.

Glancing at my bedside clock I realised I had overslept for the first time ever. Hastily I threw on my clothes, gulped down a cup of coffee and sped out of the front door. I was always at my post, by the war memorial, Bible and tracts in hand, by 9am every weekday morning, rain or shine. People were used to my being there, could set their watches by my arrival and departure; I had become a feature on their landscape.

Rather ruffled that I had allowed myself to slip just this once I straightened my collar, composed myself and raised my eyes heavenwards praying for inspiration.

Candyfloss clouds were the only interruption in the bright blue sky...

DECISION MAKING
Dennis Marshall

Candyfloss clouds were the only interruption in the bright blue sky. Beneath them was the hustle and bustle of everyday life carrying on regardless. People always found a way of ignoring the bad things that were happening and sometimes the good things as well. The city was buzzing; it was a bank holiday. Practically everybody had the day off work. The children dragged their parents around the shops trying to squeeze extra gifts out of them, and the elderly took time to sit on park benches and let the breeze blow them down memory lane. It was a day when anything could happen and anything was possible.

Birdsong was in the air at Resthead Nursing Home. To accompany it, water sprayed out from a fountain in the sunny garden. Nearby came a ripple of applause from a cricket field since the weather was ideal.

Mrs Lammas, an elderly resident at Resthead, was knitting in the shade as footsteps approached her.

'Oh Matron, it's so hot today, I shall never finish this bed jacket. I'm quite sure I shall be asleep as this pattern needs so much concentration.'

Matron smiled understandingly and joined her for a few minutes on a garden seat next to the elderly lady's wheelchair.

'The day is so lovely, Mrs Lammas, and your pattern is as beautiful. Not long now before you'll finish it!'

'How pleased I am that you like it, my dear, but you are looking worried. Have you something on your mind?'

Matron was quite touched by Mrs Lammas's concern, as the latter went on, 'I suppose the responsibility of looking after us all when several of us are out of doors is very tiring for you.'

Mrs Lammas's great friend had been Matron's mother. This is why Matron had more intimate conversations with her, especially when Mrs Lammas was by herself. What she discussed with her went no further. Mrs Lammas did not gossip and none of the other residents ever had an inkling of these facts.

'If all my residents were as thoughtful as you, we could all go camping and none of us would get lost,' Matron smiled.

The elderly lady laughed gently, she loved Matron's sense of humour. She had been a business woman running her own company for many years and she could read everyone's face as if thoughts were visible. She continued, 'May I ask you what is troubling you? Oh no,' she paused, settling her needles in her lap, 'perhaps it's private, and you've no wish to chat about it to me.'

There was a distant sharp crack, followed by some clapping. 'My grandsons play cricket and they nearly always keep their scores to themselves!' she smiled knowingly.

'I'll tell you what I'll do, Mrs Lammas,' said Matron appreciatively, 'I'll take you over to the shade of the cedar tree where you can see something of the match. It will give your eyes a rest from your pattern. Would you like to move across?'

'Now, that would be very nice but please let me pop my work into this bag. You are kind, Matron. Are you going to push me?'

'Of course, it will do me good, a bit of exercise! The staff say I spend too much time in my office, as it is. Ready? Good! Off we go!'

From the shade of the wide spreading shadow, it was just the moment for them to see a new batsman coming out. 'There, now you can count his runs! Tonight your grandson will come and tell you all about it and you can say, 'Oh, I think I know!'

'Please just sit for a moment, my dear. I know you must be frightfully busy, but you seem a little more relaxed now. Will you tell an old friend what is troubling you?'

'As always, Mrs Lammas, you are right. I sometimes think I could do with a bit of nursing myself, only don't tell anyone I've told you that!' she laughed in friendly confidence.

'There's a man once again in your life now, isn't there?' said the elderly lady. 'And I sense he's causing you some concern, I suspect.' She went on, 'I, too, had a private life, my dear, but I'm going back over fifty years. It's strange, but I remember those times better than I remember my knitting pattern!' she confessed with wry humour.

'Do you know, you are near the truth,' Matron replied, looking distantly away over to the hills.

'My dear, I can read all this in your face and ways. May I help you, if so, how can I?'

'I'm not sure if I can . . .' the younger woman paused.

'Can - what, my dear?' the elderly lady gently questioned.

'Really tell you what's troubling me. You see, I find myself pondering every so often as to whether I'm doing the right thing in the sense of making the right decision.'

'Has he asked you to marry him?' Her question came just as the spectators applauded a mighty hit.

'No, at least, not yet, but I feel it is . . . er . . . looming close, so to speak,' said the younger woman hesitatingly.

'Um! Looming close, eh! It sounds as if you're a bit apprehensive about it all,' replied her questioner.

'Mrs Lammas,' she began, 'I am. I feel at the moment life is like that. I love you all here, this is my life, my place of work, my duty, I've my house on the edge of town. Everything seems so solid, so dependable, so much part of my existence since I parted from David. Now, to change it all, rather suddenly, maybe irrevocably, even with a man who really is a lovely fellow, is making me indecisive. I guess you know only too well what I mean!'

'Love and work can go together, Sue,' she went on suddenly intimate, 'mine did, you know. It's workable, not ideal perhaps, but it is workable!' Matron listened carefully. 'John and I lived just down the road from his hospital. He used to tease me lovingly. He'd say, 'Laura, I leap out of our bed and go up there to put someone in another!' 'Ah! those were elysian days before so many changes of fortune.'

'I know,' said her listener, 'you see my problem is, how do I know whether I truly love him? I think I do. I think I can. But you see he is nearly twelve years older than I am. Does that startle you?'

'No, my dear,' she said both softly and rather surprisingly, John was nearly fifteen years my senior. Middle-aged men can be charming, reliable, safe to be with, understanding, sympathetic, lovingly appreciative, in fact, real darlings, I know!'

'Yes, I suppose they are and, can be,' Matron said slowly, as if she were walking over those faraway hills.

Do you think he would want you to give up working?'

'Well, he wants me to be happy and fulfilled. I don't want to give up. It's simply me - here! Right now, here!' she paused, then said, 'He's wonderfully fit for his age. He's great fun to be with. It's too long a tale to tell you here, but he's always sparkling company, when we are out it seems as if I've known him always. He's warm, understanding, unselfish and very firm in his opinions. Yet, he's quiet and dignified. He has two grown up children.'

'Ah! Maybe divorced, I guess?' Mrs Lammas said feelingly.

'Eh no, he's not divorced, he's a widower. His wife died three years ago and I met him in the spring of last year. But, but, but, there's so much to loving again isn't there?' Matron confessed, very deeply in thought.

'Why do you hesitate,' she said almost as if she were at one of her board meetings of yesteryear.

Matron replied, suddenly looking at her watch, 'I've written him a letter saying I don't think I'm right for him.'

'I rather think that's because you imagine you can't manage him, his home needs and your work and all of us, eh? You are torn between love and duty?'

'Well, Mrs Lammas, what would you do?' was her reply to that, just as a loud crack and a loud round of applause came from the cricket field.

'Your life is like this game of cricket,' Mrs Lammas said firmly. 'You are the next batsman, coming out to face the challenge. Keep your mind on the game as my grandsons would say - never take your eye off the ball or the fielders.'

'My dear Mrs Lammas, is life a game? For a new man in my life likens it to a game of snakes and ladders. When he gets me nearly home, I might slide down a snake and never to able to catch up a full life again!'

'Ah, my dear, but think of the joy of your next ladder!'

Sue nodded and went on to explain that Mrs Lammas was her mother's good friend and that she could often hear her mum's voice in what the wise old soul said to her in their periodic chats.

'Well, what did she advise you to do! Marry him, Sue?' Jill said rather jocularly.

Sue's reply was very thoughtful if perhaps a little indirect. 'Funnily enough we came to a study of options via snakes and ladders!' went on Sue. Jill listened with a deepening smile. 'Some we discounted,' Sue continued, 'other ideas that she had seem to point to action sooner rather than later. She knew what the risks were, so did I. Holding back a decision is a failure to act. What she really made me see was that a lack of firmness can so easily point to an opportunity for happiness to slip away.'

'Ah!' said Jill, 'that's the rub. Just what is happiness? Aren't you happy just as you are?'

'Yes, I am. Then at times, I feel I'm not!' I want to share my life. I need an arm to hold me, a voice to cheer me, encourage me. Tell me I'm right or I'm wrong. To me, solitariness is a valley between two peaks and I feel I need to climb again. But I'm not cohabiting, Jill! Marriage to me is a commitment, and I intend to keep it next time!'

'Holding back a decision is not failure, but common-sense,' put in Jill quickly, at the same time being amazed at Sue's calmness as she reasoned. 'You assess the risks,' Jill continued, 'as they say in insurance. And, if you then take out the right policy that really suits you - then that's it! Do it!'

Sue sat silently thinking.

'Give yourself three days Sue, then meet me in the Copper Kettle with your resolve watertight and your decision made!'

It was eleven o'clock on Saturday morning. Jill had taken a corner table. Sue arrived and joined her.

'Hello, Sue, fancy seeing you here! Do you come here often, as they say when boy meets girl! Now, Sue, the coffee's on me.'

'Jill, don't talk to me about boy meets girl!'

'Come now, you look as though you've lost ten pounds and found a fiver!'

'It's that man again! Do you know what he's done now?'

'Asked you to marry him!' Jill answered with the speed of light.

'If I had wings I'd fly away!' Sue said desperately.

'Calm down, Sue, what's he done?'

'He's written back. Then yesterday he sent me a really beautiful bouquet absolutely out of the blue!'

'You ought to be thrilled, my woman, over the moon, he's head over heels!'

'I wrote him three full pages. I made it clear to him, as much as I like him, that I didn't want marriage. Keep you distance and forget me! He then sends me this. Look here!'

Sue takes his letter from her handbag and gives it to Jill who holds it apprehensively and says, 'No, Sue, I ought not to!'

'Yes! Go on!'

'All right, if you insist, but where do you want me to start?'

Sue points and Jill reads.

Sue exclaims, 'See? He says again in black and white - or blue and white - asking me to marry him like a knight in shining armour leaping down from his horse!'

Jill sat for several moments longer reading, then said, 'You know, he loves you Sue, really loves you. I can't understand why you can't see that!'

'I think you're both in league,' said Sue dispassionately.

Jill replied that most certainly she was not, but then suddenly startled her friend. 'I feel I begin to know him really well now, Sue. He's a dear. He's infatuated with you. I don't know what you've said to one another but it is so obvious to me that you've lit an everlasting flame in his soul and he can't stop himself from loving you!'

'Really Jill! He's a grown man. But when he's sixty I shall not be yet fifty. It's really not on - is it? He simply can't know he loves me. How can he know?'

'When does a woman really know when she is loved, truly loved, Sue?'

Sue answered her by saying, 'That if all women knew that, the Bower of Bliss would be vastly overcrowded!'

'You may be nearer to an answer than you think,' returned Jill, 'I remember in my third year at Redbrick writing about Alexander Pope.'

'Well poetess Jilly, and what has he got to say about it?'

Jill: ''Tis not a lip or eye we beauty call
        But the joint force and full result of all!'

'So that makes me a man's magic mix, does it, Jill?'

'No, not that, but there's a great deal more to love than physical attraction. Poets know that, I know that and you should know that too. Now, listen, Sue. You are certainly the magnet drawing his attention, his passionate words and thoughts this very minute and you ask yourself why? A cool, logical why!'

Sue sat very thoughtful, sipping her coffee. 'If I knew, if only I really knew, Jill, I could stop him and then myself, because after David and I finished, I vowed and declared I never would have another emotional relationship with another man, especially one so much older than I am!'

Jill looked at her intensely. 'You know what my old gran used to say Sue? Better to be an old man's darling than a young man's slave! Come on! Life will blossom, Sue!'

Sue began to smile saying that Jill was quite a clever persuader. Jill finished her coffee. After snapping her bag shut, she turned fully to Sue saying, 'If I were in your place I'd do this! Give yourself the rest of today to think. Then either write or phone him with your final decision.'

Sue said, that she'd rather not phone that it would sound too dramatic, 'I will write to him, remember, at the outset, he wrote to me.'

'Then say, er, write something like this, that you'd be pleased to meet him again out over a meal as you've got something special to say to him. Now, if he resets your eyes aflame and your pulse racing - you know what answer to give him. For goodness sake, give it!'

'You're an incurable romantic, Jilly,' Sue said as they parted.

It was exactly three days later. Sue did ring Jill. She tried several times, but Jill was not at home so Sue left this message on her answerphone.

'It's me again. After the spadework in spring comes the autumn harvest! I'm going to marry him, Jill!'

PANIC
Joan Reeves

*Candyfloss clouds were the only interruption in the bright blue sky.
Beneath them was the hustle and bustle of everyday life carrying on
regardless. People always found a way of ignoring the bad things that
were happening and sometimes the good things as well. The city was
buzzing; it was a bank holiday. Practically everybody had the day off
work. The children dragged their parents around the shops trying to
squeeze extra gifts out of them, and the elderly took time to sit on park
benches and let the breeze blow them down memory lane. It was a day
when anything could happen and anything was possible.*

I stood at the edge of the public swimming pool. The rubber cap I
wore could not silence the acoustics. Nervously I watched the
swimmers laughing, splashing, praying they would ignore me standing,
dithering, afraid to go in.

'Come on in,' someone called, 'The water's lovely.'

I shivered, she didn't mean me did she? No, she is joined by two
friends. I needed time, I could have come with Audrey and Tom this
evening but as they were such brilliant swimmers, I would have been an
embarrassment.

Why I'm so afraid of water I don't know, after all it is a precious
commodity, think of tribes who suffer most devastating drought. Funny
I can laugh and sing in the rain but with my head immersed in water, I
panic. I can see a notice on the far wall of the baths. If I walk round
slowly I'll be able to read it.

I say it's a good thing I did read it for it says, 'Experienced
Swimmers Only'. Can you imagine what would have happened if I had
dived into this pool? I am forced to go to the other baths, which are for
juniors. The attendant gives me a funny look so I decided to go to the
pool-side cafe, for I could do with a cup of tea.

Sharing a table with a young woman who is reading a paperback, I
finish my tea, when she looks up from her book and asks, 'Have you
brought a child to swim?'

'No, I was hoping to try the water myself.'

'They have special afternoons for people your age.'

How does she know how old I am. I'm not going to let my age stop
me. Rising from the table I ask, 'Have you brought anyone?'

'Yes, I bring my little boy Tommy, he loves to play in the pool with the other toddlers.'

Suddenly all thoughts of why I was there vanished, as I thought of unsupervised children in the water. Hurriedly, I changed and made my way to the pool. For the first time that day I was alone, there was no one in or out of the pool. Alarmed I looked deep into the water. Holding the rail, I lowered myself down, and as I reached the second step I was startled by a cry.

'Help.'

I listened again.

'Help somebody. Tommy's fell in the deep end and he can't swim.'

With my heart pounding I walked quickly up the steps and ran along the length of the baths. Huddled together, I found a small group of children staring into the water.

'Quick, can you swim? Tommy's fell in,' said a small boy.

I wanted to scream, no I can't swim, but after glancing round and finding no attendant, I called out, 'Don't worry,' and taking a deep breath, plunged right into the deep end. With arms and legs flying, I felt I was learning something of the life of an octopus, and looking across to where I had left the children, they seemed miles further away.

The unfamiliar water was deep, dark and lukewarm. With a sharp cramp in my right foot, it crossed my mind that people took lessons for life saving. At last I reached out for the boy that was the cause of my predicament. I don't know how, I brought us to the water's edge, nor do I remember the attendant coming to our rescue, but as he helped me out of the water, he said, 'Whatever made you go in, a lady of your age?'

After being thanked by the boy's mother and being offered a lift home, I was feeling remarkably well. Refusing the lift, I found myself sitting with some self-satisfaction, on the 47 bus, homeward bound.

As I went up my garden path, my neighbour, Mrs Davis greeted me. 'Your daughter called today. I told her I hadn't seen you go out.'

'I've been swimming.'

'Swimming?' she cried in disbelief. 'But I thought you were afraid of water?'

'Not anymore,' I said, proudly.

'And did you go right into the water?'

Closing my door gently, I replied, 'I most certainly did.'

DARK PASSAGE
Glenwyn Peter Evans

Candyfloss clouds were the only interruption in the bright blue sky. Beneath them was the hustle and bustle of everyday life carrying on regardless. People always found a way of ignoring the bad things that were happening and sometimes the good things as well. The city was buzzing; it was a bank holiday. Practically everybody had the day off work. The children dragged their parents around the shops trying to squeeze extra gifts out of them, and the elderly took time to sit on park benches and let the breeze blow them down memory lane. It was a day when anything could happen and anything was possible.

Joan Goddard Jones relaxed, keeping a careful eye trained on the old woman, a down-and-out, sitting next to her on the park bench; silently, judging, weighing her up.

Dirty, horrible, smelly old bitch, ran the contemptible thoughts residing within her head. Wants a good flamin' scrub.

All at once, the old woman glanced; an estranged look flared her eye; the fiery, blank stare made Joan shudder, tingling, a morbid, disintegrating feeling that she, the old woman, was reading her mind.

'Wan' some luv?' she asked in a low, cold, gravel voice, knocking back some thick, black liquid.

'Tea?' mumbled Joan, licking her dry lips. 'On a hot summer's day?'

The old woman narrowed her eyes, nodding her head. A weird sneer spread across her face. 'Scared of catching somefin', luvvy?'

A lump formed in Joan's throat, tongue-tied as to how to respond. 'No,' she assured her, laconically, 'Why should I be?' Taking a cautious sip, then knocking it back.

'Real tea leaves, these ar' luvvy,' smiled the toothless tramp.

Joan choked. Get away from me, vile creature! she thought.

'All in good time,' snorted she, squinting her right eye.

Joan froze, body tensing, her soft, sanguine face numbed. 'Can you read minds?' she asked, pathetically, passing the cup with a shaking hand. In a fleeting glance, a tinge of red flashed into the old woman's eyes as she snatched the cup from Joan's delicate hand, twisting it, quickly, forcing open the palm.

'I can see that you are a 'fine' judge of character,' she snapped vehemently. 'At least, you like to think you are. Niggardy bitch!'

Joan, choking upon the unstrained tea leaves, that seemed to stay stubbornly on her tongue, snatched back her hand, fiercely. It was enough to make the old woman grin, wickedly.

'I've already seen your palm,' she revealed, passively, pointing a small bent, withered finger, gazing deeply into the mug.

'Please,' murmured Joan, looking for a quick escape, 'I can't take anymore of that horrid tea . . .'

'Who said anything about drinking?' barked the old woman, in short, gruff, staccato clips. 'I'm going to tell you somefin' 'bout yerself. Never delve in somefin' you don't know nofin' 'bout. It's a dark passage . . .'

'What, from the tea leaves?' scoffed Joan, sceptically.

'Oh,' returned the old woman, mildly, flashing a toothless grin. 'Everything I see is in the leaves, deary. As well as your palm!'

'Rubbish!' exclaimed Joan, vehemently, rising on the defensive . . .

'Beware of the Dark Passage.'

Joan rudely turned her back on her, hoping the old bitch would disappear. By the time she took a deep, quivering breath, she had. How weird, she thought, alighting the park bench, warily, looking for her. The lady had vanished.

By noon, the day was absolutely brilliant. The sun was scorching. the sky was now a vaulting, deep, sapphire blue with just the odd wisp of puffy clouds, with a light, cool breeze that seemed to pick up the moment she walked, pushing her, rigidly, in the opposite direction she wanted to go.

Obliviously, she was lost to the world, mesmerised within her own. She had trailed to a semi-circle of woods, wondering desperately; wondering how on earth she came to be here?

Across the way, an invisible horse neighed. All at once, from out of the woods, the charger appeared in all its glorious splendour, bucking, rearing, reined masterfully by a knight in shining armour.

Nostrils flaring, it began to gallop across the field towards her. Joan stood, motionless, gaping, wondering for the life of her as to what to make of it all.

The warrior, fluttering a pennant of crimson red, unsheathed his sword, dripping with blood, shrilling as he swept the air with it, charging thunderously.

The moment before impact, with a tremendous humph, Joan dived for the ground. The air was still, and profoundly calm. The only thing left beside her was the crimson pennant, soaked in blood . . Nerves raw and on edge, she stood aghast, trembling.

'What significance,' she asked her friend, pale and sombre, 'Did the words *war'tah* mean?'

'Nothing,' Jean Swayid informed her, with a frown, pouring out another drink.

Joan nervously relaxed on the veranda, overlooking Sidney Harbour silhouetted against the bright, blue flamed sky.

'You just experienced a very, vivid daymare.'

'Daymare?' levelled Joan, with an air of oafish surprise.

'Yes,' she went on to explain, considering herself to be an expert on such subjects as the occult, witchcraft, dreams, as also a practising clairvoyant; returning with the two iced drinks, clinking inside the glass. 'According to the book I'm reading now, a daymare is the opposite of a nightmare; eyes being fully dilated while they're really in a very deep stupor. Only a few people ever experience it.'

'Huh, amazing? So you're saying I dreamt everything?'

'Believe you me,' murmured Jean, convincingly. 'I've read worse. Dreams have been known to spell out sublime messages.'

'My knight in shining armour?' said Joan, chuckling dryly, 'I think it's telling me I need to get a life.'

'Let me explain. For instance; have you ever had that dream where one minute you're strolling along, then, what! You trip over a brick or something, and your whole body violently jerks and heaves until you're lying awake, staring at nothing but the inky blackness?'

'Yeah, I suppose,' returned her friend, managing a nervous laugh, chilling the cool glass against her reddish complexion.

'So, you see how imaginary it is then, don't you? And didn't the blood-soaked pennant disappear before you could pick it up?'

'Of course,' she declared, 'How stupid of me!'

Casually, Joan walked the one and a half kilometres to her favourite place, the Sidney Harbour. There was nothing in the world that gave her as much greater pleasure, tranquillity and peace of mind, than watching the many different kinds of craft that sailed there. It was serene, beautiful, and so enchanting-like.

Below a sun-scorched sky, she sat back upon a wooden bench, thinking of everything she'd done throughout her life. The boyfriends she'd dumped. The lively pranks she'd played while at high school, and the friends she once knew. Not one of them were as close as Jean though; the aborigine girl that everyone disliked . . .

Disliked? It seemed almost incredible now that anyone could ever dislike her. She was the best looking girl in the whole school of year sixteen, with a great, easy-outgoing personality. So what if she was a dyke? Joan smiled. Lesbianism was a misunderstood thing back then, closing her eyes to the blissful sound of blaring, hooting ships.

I've always loved the call of the sea, she mused, her thoughts swirling her head. What makes people want to go to sea . . .? Drifting to the rhythmic, hypnotic splashing of the foam crested waves as they gently lapped the wooden pier.

The planks moved beneath her feet, just a gentle roll at first. She'd never known that to happen before, opening her eyes.

To the right, in the distance stood the Cape Hermes lighthouse; brilliant, dazzling white pitched against jagged, dark cliffs.

Something was wrong. Something did not register with her brain. Joan sat, numbly, observing the fashion of the people leisurely walking by. They were dressed differently. Almost old fashioned-like?

Suddenly, her eyes were borne to a new concept. She was aboard a ship, ocean bound. But which ship? How? And where were they bound?

The five funnel, ten thousand ton passenger ship, vibrated at a steady thirteen knots. Joan became frantic. Had she been shanghaied and stowed aboard when sleeping?

She shot up, deck planks flitting beneath her plump, lined body as the hustle and bustle of everyday life continued, unabated.

A rasping, cold, ominous feeling began to nag her soul. She saw people talking, lips moving, with no sound coming out. She called out frantically, 'What ship is this?' But all she got in return was the deep, foreboding shrill of salted wind, below a purple-black, angry sky.

Hurriedly, in search of answers, she scoured the music lounge, the minstrels' gallery. But no one took any notice as she repeated her question, breathlessly, over and over again.

They're all deaf? She squirmed, pushing back the heavy curtains, clambering the plush settees with tuckered backs, not noticing that the potted palms were swaying, and the concealed lights, flashing. She ran amidships, where the ferocious wind, whistled and howled. The ship shuddered, juddered,; bolts that held the planks in place flew in the air; wind-torn crests of mighty breakers smashed its darkened bows on a blazing, ripping trail of destruction as the ship swayed and rolled; for a scary moment, it almost turned, turtle over.

Joan, eyes squinting, sweating fear, shrieked hysterically under a mountainous swirl of blinding spray. The tempo picked up, hellishly. The ship dived, listing to port at a forty-five degree angle. Joan screamed, rolling the splintered deck before the mighty ship bottomed out, troughing herself into a self-righting position.

The gale blowing violently, did not let up and Joan scrambled to the lifeline for all she was worth. Anything wooden, was battered and blown away; water lashed amidships, tearing at beams and planks. Rain stung like red-hot lead shot as it spat in her face. There was no time to cry. She had to get out . . .Get out of this dark passage.

'Dark passage,' she exclaimed, as the old lady reappeared, eyes glaring savagely, snorting:

'You did not heed the warning!' before she vanished once more.

Joan fought, hurled and plummeted her body towards the bridge. Three hundred metre breakers beat her back as the ship dived, prow first into an unfathomable, deep black hole, only to be jostled by the wicked elements and thrusted skyward bound by the next; then down . . .

Down . . Down . . . into the black abyss of no return . . . Joan remembered the ship's name. Whispering it to her friend Jean Swayid, as she gurgled and choked . . .

'*Waratah!*' exclaimed Jean, eyes bulging in their sockets, bolting out of her sleep. 'It was the *SS Waratah!*' remembering all too well the story of the dream and vision seen by Mr Claude G Sawyer, before the Blue Anchor Line passenger ship, disappeared, twelve miles off the coast of Africa . . . In the year 1909.

'But why Joan? Why did the knight come back for Joan?' Then it hit her, the sublime warning . . . Like a bolt of lightning from out of the blue . . . J G Jones, her best friend, never existed! She was an illusion. There was no such person . . . And if there was no such person as Joan

Goddard Jones, then that meant it was I, Jean Swayid that took that nefarious Dark Passage!

Why?

'Because I summoned up the lost souls of the doomed ship *SS Waratah!* Me!' Turning to face the exploding, thundering, demonic wrath. Her executioner.

THE MAGICAL, MYSTERY BOAT TRIP
Connie Garrard

Candyfloss clouds were the only interruption in the bright blue sky. Beneath them was the hustle and bustle of everyday life carrying on regardless. People always found a way of ignoring the bad things that were happening and sometimes the good things as well. The city was buzzing; it was a bank holiday. Practically everybody had the day off work. The children dragged their parents around the shops trying to squeeze extra gifts out of them, and the elderly took time to sit on park benches and let the breeze blow them down memory lane. It was a day when anything could happen and anything was possible.

In fact, it turned out to be a day filled with the unexpected. There would be a strange symmetry between tragedy and wonderment - a day that was to change my life forever!

Now, before I enlighten you about my experience, I should really introduce myself. My name is Holly Davis. I'm a humble graphic designer who is quite good at her trade - so they say! I love my job and enjoy dreaming up and creating designs for various advertising companies and CD covers for up and coming rock stars. My close circle of friends refer to me as Holly the Happy Hippy! They all think I'm stuck in a 1970's time warp as I'm always listening to music of that decade - anything from Bowie to Kate Bush. I wear my hair long and straight, and yes! you've guessed correctly, I adore love beads and the colour purple - but hey! it's the 21st century, who cares? Anything goes, well, practically anything! One has to be politically correct these days, which isn't easy at times!

I certainly remember that bank holiday quite well. It was August 2002. I needed to pay a visit to my local town centre in Durham. It's a very nice place. I wanted to purchase another tube of burnt sienna, in order to complete my latest graphic creation. Unfortunately the atmosphere was extremely stifling in the shopping precinct. The place was swarming with all kinds of people, oh yes, all the stereotypes were there. I could hear shrill cries coming from spoilt toddlers having temper tantrums and tiny tots who had no sense of direction, ending up under my feet - well, almost!

Mr and Mrs Bloggs were there of course, rowing as per usual. Mr Bloggs obviously not enjoying the pleasure of shopping, let alone the huge reduction in his bank balance, due to Mrs Bloggs' enthusiasm and expensive taste in the soft furnishings department. All the spotty teenage population seemed to be present, armed with plenty of attitude and their mobile phones. Oh, and not all the elderly were enjoying their time on the park bench - oh no! Some decided to brave it out amongst the rabble, on such a busy day. It was hard for me to gauge how fast to walk! I would try to keep up with the flow, dodging the youths, texting their boyfriends, but soon came to an abrupt halt after suddenly being confronted by a frail old boy armed with his walking stick. Now please, don't get me wrong, I have nothing against the elderly. It will come to most of us eventually. This gentleman was probably quite dynamic and a real lady-killer in his youth. However, a slight breeze could blow him over. These folk should perhaps go shopping at quieter, safer times if possible. It would certainly help me to keep my sanity and maintain a normal pulse rate. Negotiating these people in the precinct can be quite a task!

I was not far from my beloved artshop, when I started to have some problems with my eyesight. Was one of my visual migraines coming on? I could see big golden flashes before my eyes. These flashes soon turned into zigzags. I started to panic. This only made things worse. The zigzags just turned larger until they united in shimmery, circular patterns. Normally, a slender cigar would have calmed me down, but not in this instance, as I was having difficulty breathing too! I thought, oh hell! What's happening? The picture was breaking up in front of me. I couldn't breathe at all by this stage.

Now the next thing that happened was weird! I semed to be floating up above, almost touching the ceiling, looking down upon myself. From this vantage point I observed that I was being surrounded by a lot of concerned people. All the curious busybodies who love to be at the scene of an accident, or special incident, were there. Yes indeed! They were certainly having a good look and hoping for an eventful show! It just dawned on me that I was having an out-of-body experience. I'd heard people discussing this subject in the past, but never, in a million years, thought that I would have one! Wow! I pondered for a while and said to myself, am I dead? - I must be! I noticed that people were now prodding my earthly body and doing all sorts of curious things to me. It looked as if my heart had stopped! Hello, who's this? I can remember thinking. It was possibly a paramedic who, by now, had come to my aid. I was fascinated by his waist length hair, which was tied back in a ponytail. Possibly it was because of the hippy instinct coming out in me - all that flower power man!

Now what was happening? I felt that I was a floating soul who was being whisked away! Then I found myself in the tunnel that people seem to refer to, and yes! There was an amazing light. It had a somewhat hypnotic affect on me. I felt quite relaxed, as if in a state of transcendental meditation. My body, or shall I say my soul, was soon to be gently thrust out of the tunnel.

I found myself in the most beautiful courtyard. Could this be heaven? I wasn't at all sure, I didn't quite feel it was, but felt hopeful. My attention drifted to a sight that tickled my sense of humour. In one section of the courtyard was a group men who looked familiar to me. They were sitting amongst a stunning array of poppies. To my disbelief I realised who they were. I could see many rock gods! However, two of them were seated at a magnificent white Steinway grand piano. They were working on a new composition. It was Bolan and Mercury! Could this be a fantastic dream I was having? I then noticed a handsome, dark haired man passing in the background. He had a well defined square jaw line and eyes that were full of mischief. He also had a dangerous, but magnetic aura about his persona. I think it was Morrison.

At the opposite end of the courtyard someone else was gaining people's attention, there was a man seated at a celeste, playing the most ornate music. He was playing at such a rapid, rapid tempo, that it really excited his audience. What a showman - what an extrovert. 'Was it the boy genius - Mozart?' and could that be a large 16th century English king, laughing heartily and marvelling at his skill? This was so uncanny. Suddenly Martin Luther King walked by. He was accompanied by Ghandi. Then two philosophers, engaged in deep conversation also passed by. Had I just see Socrates and Plato? I was certainly doing a lot of reasoning with myself at this point! Was this a glorified waiting room filled with souls of the dead? I was confused.

Suddenly I spotted a rather ornate archway. It was covered in delicate flowers. I witnessed vivid shades I had not seen in my paintbox, or anywhere else for that matter. I wondered where this archway would lead. Standing nearby was a very happy, young couple.

They looked so in love and glad to be reunited. It was Elizabeth and Bertie. My curiosity got the better of me and I went to see what was yonder.

It was fantastic. I saw an incredible blue lake. It sparkled, as if covered with diamonds. Then my eyes fell upon a rather plain, but quaint sailing boat. There was a man already sitting in it, but with his back to me. He had waist length hair and was wearing a loose, white garment. Steering the boat was a sturdy looking man, with a healthy, ruddy complexion. His hair was dark and curly and he had a matty beard. He looked like a fisherman. I thought perhaps this man with the kind, smiling eyes could tell me where I was. I resigned myself to the fact that I was dead! The man laughed loudly with much resonance and his eyes were twinkling more than ever. He said

'Holly, you've come too soon. Go back and I'll see you later. My companion and I have decisions to make!' Everything changed again. A swirly, pink mist covered the boat scene.

Now, all I could sense was a silent, but peaceful veil of darkness. This was soon followed by a feeling of great pain. I thought my head would explode. I then saw red in front of my eyes and the silhouette of a man leaning over me. Then gradually all the normal colours returned. This angel had the most amazing eyes which were as blue as sapphires. He had a gentle, reassuring manner. His soft beard and moustache were most becoming. He said 'Hi! My name is Jason, I'm a paramedic. We thought we'd lost you, but you're going to be fine now!'

I was too dazed to comment! Jason then winked at me and whispered something softly in my ear. I think he said

'Don't worry, you will have your magical, mystery boat trip!'

FROM UNDER A STONE . . .

Di Bagshawe

Candyfloss clouds were the only interruption in the bright blue sky. Beneath them was the hustle and bustle of everyday life carrying on regardless. People always found a way of ignoring the bad things that were happening and sometimes the good things as well. The city was buzzing; it was a bank holiday. Practically everybody had the day off work. The children dragged their parents around the shops trying to squeeze extra gifts out of them, and the elderly took time to sit on park benches and let the breeze blow them down memory lane. It was a day when anything could happen and anything was possible.

A finger of sun eventually found its way round the maze of the arches and poked itself into my eye - it wasn't welcome. I needed sleep, God knows what they had been up to down on the left. Someone must have been on a bad trip, I heard sounds of dragging as something was removed from our row of 'semi-detacheds'. One of the rules of the Freedom Lovers, as this lot called themselves, was no casualties on the doorstep, no one wanted the Old Bill or do-gooders asking questions and evicting them.

I needed a pee, so dragged myself down to the public loos on the other side of the railway arches. Phew! I'd have almost gone home to use somewhere nicer, and the bright day made it even more sordid. With all my bits and pieces strung round I teetered on the edge of a pile of vomit, wet my flannel at the basin, no need to turn on the tap it was constantly dripping, and barricaded the door to strip down. No locks of course. No mirrors either, but at least the condom dispenser had a shiny surface.

I was really hitting a low today, how could the once smart PA be me? What I needed was some of that sun to give the crawled-out-from-under-a-stone look a bit of a flush. Scrabbling round in the bottom of my bundles in the hopes of finding enough cash to get some breakfast I met something nasty . . . seriously nasty! That settled it, I'd crash out in the park and hope to find somewhere to spread out my things where I wouldn't be moved on.

When you're carrying your all on a bright summer's day, you don't want to be mingling with people in shirt sleeves, minis and spaghetti straps. I wasn't just sweating, I was dissolving, and despite my so-called wash I could smell myself. At least it gave me some space on the pavement.

At last the riverside gardens came in sight, and it was all I could do to shuffle over the road to get to them. A few minutes of recce to make sure there weren't any officials about, and I slunk into blessed shade to recover, a hidden patch of grass remembered from happier times.

Air! I was almost panting like a dog with the combination of fresh air to breath (bar a slight pollution from the adjoining road) and the joy of offloading the various bags from my shoulders.

I must have dropped off, a chopper following the river line made me start. Time meant little unless I was trying to get a bed in the shelter, but my empty stomach was having a percussion concert all on its own. Once again I tackled my bags pulling out dingy clothes, knife, fork and spoon, a metal mug and plastic plate. The makings of a roll-up, only the tobacco pouch was empty and the papers hopelessly stuck and crumpled. Then the horror, remains, very dead remains, of all things of a tuna mayo sandwich. Even to my well deadened olfactory powers it was puke making. I flung it into bushes as far as I could, hoping it wouldn't give the local wildlife collective ptomaine poisoning, turned the bag inside out and began scraping with bunches of grass trying to hold my breath. When it was reduced to a greasy stain I left it in the sun hoping to bake out the lingering pong. There was a drinking fountain somewhere in these gardens, would there be people there, dared I wash out pants and a bra?

I stuffed my 'luggage' under a bush, not that anyone in their right mind would have wanted to nick any of it, and clutching a handful of decrepit garments, I began stalking that fountain with all the care of an Indian Scout. Bless the guardian angel of all vagrants, the coast was clear, no offices open and lunchtime for mums with small kids. I stripped off my T-shirt and began rubbing the clothes in the water, sun-warmed in the basin, blissfully cool from the fountain. The garments as clean as I could get them I held myself over the water and splashed and rubbed what I could reach in turn. I was so absorbed in this pleasurable occupation I completely forgot the public nature of my wash house.

A gang of youths slouched up, mixed lot with a variety of hairstyles from dreadlocks to shaven in patterns, pieced in every conceivable place, pants sliding off hips in lengths from under shoes (universally trainers) to cut-offs, and all with chains slung from pockets and flying shirts in the light breeze. Every face had a leer of sorts, and one began walking appraisingly round me like a cattle auctioneer, one began a slow hand clap and 'get it off . . .' and another two started to discuss the deficiencies or good points on view. The fifth just stood and gazed mouth open, must be a mum's boy with no chance to see a centre spread. The cattle one started to kick my wet washing and I went ballistic, screaming words recently added to my vocabulary on the streets, and at the same time frantically pulling my shirt on again.

A middle-aged couple were now in sight at the far end of the park and looked our way in enquiry and some nervousness, this was enough for the gang to take off by mutual assent still commenting as they went.

In case the couple did come up I hastily gathered up my belongings and fled to the shelter of the bushes where I'd left my things. I was more than a little shattered by the episode and again wished I had the money for a cuppa. To calm myself I started to hang my laundry on the bushes around hoping no one would come that way.

'Hullo! My lucky day is it?' and a fellow traveller came round into view.

'Push off, I got here first,' was my welcome to him.

'Now dear, no unpleasantness, public place and I've been coming here for more years than you've had hot dinners.'

I could well believe it, he appeared to look after himself, everything round him organised, spoke well too, what had brought him to be a gentleman of the road?

'Wish you wouldn't talk about hot dinners,' and to my horror my voice sounded really childishly peevish.

'Hungry are you? I was in the shelter last night, got a nice cuppa and bread and jam before I left.'

'Alright for some, I'm skint and had no luck on the scrounge last night.'

'Need to know the ropes that's all, I work my patch on a strict rota, and there's usually something coming in, food and drink if not cash.'

I busied myself shaking out my bits turning them to the sun.

'Nothing like drying in the open, I can remember my mum bringing in the sheets after a good blow, the smell of the outdoors, I used to open her airing cupboard and sniff, grass and things and lavender she put under the lining paper. Funny nostalgic smell lavender, old ladies, nice things. Now it's in the health shops and all aromatherapy.'

'Were you brought up in the country then? I've always been a townie myself, country smells don't appeal all that much, but I do love the sea. We went each year . . . not so much the sand in the sandwiches, funny I thought that was where they got their name, but blackberries on the clifftop, suntan oil - you know. Mum used to always take ginger biscuits, said they warmed our tums, the hard kind you had to dip in your cup when you began to lose your teeth . . .' at which point my tum gave a mega gurgle. He grinned,

'That gave you away, what have you eaten today?'

When I told him nothing he started clucking like an old hen about feeding up at my age. Why hadn't I gone to get some food instead of lying about in the park?

'Here, are those flimsies dry enough? Well shove them in your bags and we'll go and look for something, I know a place or two, and if all else fails I did quite well on the handouts yesterday and I'd be delighted to entertain a young lady like you.'

Not exactly the escort I'd been used to, but well meaning, so I said that it would be nice to have company and thank you.

My companion having proved his expertise by helping me pack, we set off. He poked his head into a cabman's pull-in, the owner looked up and jerked a thumb towards the rear, and we dutifully walked round to the kitchen door.

'Good to see you Dave, how've you been keeping? That lout of a lad of mine's not turned up and I'm run off my feet with the fine weather . . . how about cleaning up that stack there in return for a fry-up for you and the young lady?'

'No sooner said than done Jim, you're always a pal.'

With two of us working the greasy pile diminished and once again my companion proved himself methodical and efficient.

'Been a sailor' he said 'no room for muddle below decks.'

The buzz in the cafe died down and Jim reappeared,

'Reckon we could all do with a break, and we'll hear the bell if anyone comes in. I put three platefuls in the warmer when I did the last order.'

Never, but never, has food tasted so good, though almost too much for my unaccustomed stomach. We finished, washed our three dishes, then sat on the kitchen step in the late sun with cuppas in hand.

Someone walked by, walked back, hesitated.

'Good grief Megan, is it you?'

Squinting in the sun I saw Alan from the old office.

'What the hell's going on, you just disappeared and we've all been looking for you.'

'It all got too much, Chris bringing that little bitch into the flat, redundancy on top of it, I just dropped out of the rat race.'

'Ann and I collected your things from the flat, and now they've installed a new system the contracts are pouring in, you were one of the brightest sparks in the office, they'll have you back like a shot. Won't you come home with me, Ann would be over the moon to know you're safe.'

What had I got to lose, the bright day had shown me the sordidness and my incompetence in the wandering life. I turned to Jim,

'You've brought me luck today, thank you.'

'I knew there was something under the surface Megan, make it work this time.'

Hitching his bags onto his back Dave called a goodbye to Jim, and strolled off whistling.

Alan hailed a taxi and feeling like Cinderella I dumped my bags in Jim's dustbin, and got in.

THE JUDGEMENT
Don Woods

Candyfloss clouds were the only interruption in the bright blue sky. Beneath them was the hustle and bustle of everyday life carrying on regardless. People always found a way of ignoring the bad things that were happening and sometimes the good things as well. The city was buzzing; it was a bank holiday. Practically everybody had the day off work. The children dragged their parents around the shops trying to squeeze extra gifts out of them, and the elderly took time to sit on park benches and let the breeze blow them down memory lane. It was a day when anything could happen and anything was possible.

But both young and old were blissfully unaware, that life on this most pleasant of days from this day forth, for the whole of humanity was about to change.

It was some eight months later, that Paula Page, senior nurse at the local maternity home, noticed as she checked future admissions to her ward, that no beds had been booked. Assuming there must be some mistake she double-checked. But it was so; not one bed had been booked after the next two weeks, which meant that the ward would then be empty. Alarmed she contacted the hospital administrator, who suggested that they should offer their empty beds to other hospitals that maybe had a bed shortage. But to their amazement they found that each hospital they contacted was in the same quandary. No admission had been booked.

The minister for health was informed. Who after checking with health authorities throughout the United Kingdom placed an immediate ban on this information being released to anybody, especially the press, until he had presented the result of his enquiries to the Government.

Meanwhile in doctors' surgeries throughout the UK, young couples desperate to have children were being given the bad news that the husband's sperm was infertile. It wasn't until the various laboratories were inundated with samples for checking that it was realised that there was a serious national problem. Which within hours of urgent global telephone calls, proved to be a world problem. Apparently all males the world over had become infertile. The best brains were set to work around the clock, to find the reason for the crisis. But as the next three months went by, an even bigger shock was to come. It was found that older people were dying prematurely. Not in any pain or through an obvious illness, but simply dying in their sleep. Which meant that most of the world's best scientists, who maybe could have solved the problem, were now either dead or dying. The world panicked as it was realised that children that had recently been born, would be the last humans on earth unless a cure for the crisis could be found.

Within two months crematoriums and churches couldn't handle the amount of dead. Bodies were being stored in warehouses and homes everywhere, creating a massive health risk. Until finally the Government declared Martial Law and ordered mass burials regardless of religion, much to the fury of the various church leaders.

Months turned to years, and still no cure was found. Radiation, global warming, pesticides, depleted ozone layer, nuclear fallout, were all blamed, but then someone realised that animals were still having their young. Why were they not affected? There was chaos everywhere. Industry was grinding to a halt as operators of machines died. Insurance companies were going bankrupt, unable to pay out the massive amount of claims against them. Even the armed forces were in disarray, as personnel deserted in droves to be with their families or loved ones. Seeing no point in being in an army when there would soon be no one to fight anyway.

Twenty-two years passed and Dr Matthew Selwin, one of the last children to be born, even though so young was now the chief government scientist in overall charge of the United Kingdom teams searching for a cure. He was having lunch with his twin brother Giles. Giles was a highly respect member of the clergy, and had his own sermons broadcast on national radio every Sunday morning, which even before the crisis had a tremendous following. However now his radio station was inundated with letters from millions of new converts, from the rapidly dwindling population. Who, getting no answers from their own religious leaders, were turning to his no nonsense ordinary language way of preaching the Lord's word. Giles was now pleading with his brother for some good news to give to his congregation the approaching Sunday. But it was not forthcoming. And his brother still could not explain why, when sperm was brought from a sperm bank back alive, died as soon as it was introduced to the female egg.

That night in his study he read his bible hoping for God's guidance. But nothing seemed to help.

'Lord, don't fail me now,' he cried throwing the book down in frustration. The bible hit the desk and fell open. On going to close it he saw the heading Genesis. Whether this happened by divine intervention he did not know, but he sat and started to read, as he had done so many times before, about the Garden of Eden. And in the dawn's early light he knew what he was going to tell his listeners.

To try to calm rioting and panic that was rife throughout the nation, the government had decided that he would broadcast not on the Radio, but on national television.

It was with a heavy heart that he spoke into the camera.

'For many years I have preached the gospel to you. But today I realise that my prepared speech is useless. So I will put this to one side and tell you my thoughts on the current crisis.

The bible tells of many great catastrophes that have occurred on earth in the past seemingly sent down as a punishment on mankind. But now we have the final ultimate catastrophe that is visited on us and we only have ourselves to blame. I want you to imagine that I built a great garden, and filled it with flowers, plants, and trees of all descriptions. Then to make my garden even more beautiful I filled it with animals of every kind. And in my garden I am well pleased. Then into my garden came a blight that started to destroy my beautiful garden. Then I would be angry and destroy that blight so that my garden would be beautiful once more.' He paused.

Well that is happening now to us! Our world was created as a beautiful garden, and mankind was also included. But man in his selfishness and greed has become the blight on that beautiful garden. So the Lord who created this garden has decided to remove that blight. All our older folk are dying prematurely; no more babies are being born. We are the last of the human race. We alone are to blame. Like the dinosaurs we will soon be no more. Our lives and the generation before us have despoiled the paradise called Earth. What with wars, the building of great sprawling cities, and now pollution that is now poisoning the very air we breathe. Then we go to church each Sunday to pray for forgiveness. My own brother said to me, that if he gave me a present he would not expect me to spend every Sunday the rest of my life thanking him for it. No he would much rather see me put his present to good use. Well that's what we should have done with our present, which is the gift of life. We should have used it to make the Lord's garden even more beautiful. Not as we have done, by killing off the animals and destroying forests, taking lush landscapes to build beautiful cathedrals, churches, palaces and so on. Beautiful to who? Only to mankind. Not the animals, fish, birds and plant life that is now extinct. Look around his garden at the derelict factories we could not be bothered to pull down, the devastation and desolation caused by wars, can you blame our creator for wanting his garden back to how it was? And finally I say to you. If there is a chance of us being forgiven for the damage we have done we are going to have to earn it. Clean up the air, clean up the land, and clean up the seas. The answer is in our hands before it is too late. Let us give him back his beautiful garden.'

The picture faded.

Thirty years had passed and the Elite Squad moved from building to building setting their charges. Factories, warehouses, schools, hospitals, churches, that were no longer used had to be levelled to the ground, denying shelter to the thousands of starving and savage cats and dogs that roamed the streets and countryside, attacking anything that moved. People had moved from outlying villages and smaller towns to the inner cities, for protection and the few services that were still working. Food could be grown in abundance in the countryside, but could not be harvested because of the dogs. So farms were taken under state control and protected by the Elite police. Feeding the people had never been a problem, for as factories and stores had closed due to the deaths of the workers, their stocks had been brought to state warehouses for distribution when needed.

Another five years passed and the search for a cure had been given up. Also here and abroad populations were dwindling fast due to starvation and disease.

Matthew was driving back from the North, where for the last two months he had been overseeing the cleaning up work of the people. Now, motorways, roads, railways, no longer sprawled across the countryside. Skylines were now as nature intended. Ships had been taken out to sea and sunk, oil rigs shut down. Now only sail was used. Cars, trucks, buses now illegal to use the world over, had been scrapped and dumped down worked out mines or buried in landfill sites. But he was angry. If there was a God, then why was he destroying mankind? He parked and looked over the lush landscape before him and thought of the good and bad things that man had done. Then realisation came to him. Man deserved this fate. He had been given a chance to build a world of love and beauty but had made a world of greed and avarice. As night came he stared up at the crystal clear sky that was no longer polluted and he made this prayer.

'I know you are watching us. I know you care about your world. But did you never make a mistake? We are only a speck of dust on the ground you walk on, but we have learned our lesson. Please give us once more the charge of caring for your world.'

And the watcher heard.

Ann Selwin was bursting with joy. Today was her birthday and the day that Matthew would be back after his trip away. And what tremendous news she had for him, It had happened six weeks ago when she had started being sick in the mornings. On asking Gile's wife Sue for some aspirin thinking she had flu, she found that Sue was suffering the same symptoms. Although it was deemed impossible for them to have children, there was not a woman alive who had not read books on childbirth. And the symptoms were those of morning sickness. Frantic phone calls around her married friends told they were not the only two. Old maternity wards were opened up to make sure. And to their joy the crisis was over, and the few of mankind that were left were being given another chance. Giles on being told the news fell to his knees in prayer saying 'On behalf of your New World, thank you Lord. We will not let you down.'

And the watcher heard.

CRUMBLE BEE'S EXCITING DAY
Peter Asher

Candyfloss clouds were the only interruption in the bright blue sky. Beneath them was the hustle and bustle of everyday life carrying on regardless. People always found a way of ignoring the bad things that were happening and sometimes the good things as well. The city was buzzing; it was a bank holiday. Practically everybody had the day off work. The children dragged their parents around the shops trying to squeeze extra gifts out of them, and the elderly took time to sit on park benches and let the breeze blow them down memory lane. It was a day when anything could happen and anything was possible.

Poorly Boy sighed and switched off the cassette player. Even one of his favourite short stories couldn't get him in the mood for the fun day ahead. All those people, the thought of, he didn't like at all. Not for a moment would he have spoken to them both, though, for he liked to see the happiness in their eyes which reminded him of himself sometimes when he looked in the mirror on a happy day when all the world was, if not seaside, then a poorly toy made better.

For actually Poorly Boy hated the seaside on a hot, people swarming summer's day. But Mum and Dad loved it he knew, so he pretended to be excited at the prospect. This pretend started the evening before when he persuaded Daddy Springy to pretend to be excited at the prospect. Also Baby Kenneth, Nelly and Little Sheeps, all acting excited for none of them wanted to go either, strange as it seems.

And in the car, stuck in the jam, baking in the heat of the excited sun on its way to the seaside and streaming in through the car windows - Poorly Boy and his staff bravely played how delighted we are. Or rather one did and one didn't.

Dad had whispered to Mum last minute before setting off that Crumble Bee had been grumbling to him how he never got to get out of looking after the hospital. Poorly Boy informed Dad previous to this not only how excited he was, but that the others had begged him to take them too, so his entire staff was going.

'Great,' not too convincingly mumbled Dad.

Then Dad had gone to Mum saying

'Sue he's taking the lot with him - that's all we need. He'll lose one of them in the crush on the sands and we'll spend all day trying to find

Baby Kenneth or whoever gets lost. I've an idea might change Poorly Boy's mind.'

So Crumble Bee had complained to Dad at just the right time, Poorly Boy agreeing it would make a nice change for the bee.

'But he's a bit grouchy Dad, even when he's in a good mood, so it's best we take Daddy Springy as he won't dare fall out with him.' (This fact was to prove untrue). Dad nodded a smug sort of nod.

Poorly Boy just had time to tell the others they wouldn't be going to the seaside and they all clapped their paws, trunks and ears and ran about quietly cheering. A bar of chocolate and some dusty peanuts, (the same ones always used for similar leavings), was placed on the bed, together with some comics and a jigsaw puzzle of Hampton Court Maze, so they wouldn't get bored. As none of them were into computers - and Poorly Boy wasn't too keen either, he felt he needn't warn Little Sheeps, as the eldest in charge, to be careful when plugging in. Baby Kenneth sat smiling with a lapful of dull, dusty, red peanuts.

Poorly Boy kissed each in turn and within an hour or so they were excitedly looking for somewhere to park on an exciting stretch of crowded road along the sea front at Sandhill On The Rocks. It had been a happy journey.

Crumble Bee had a blister forming on his left antenna; the one being broken when he was first found.

'It often gives him trouble, Mum.'

This blister got bigger and bigger as the sun, eager to get to the seaside, sat in the window nearest Crumble Bee and hitched a ride from this position never moving away until they arrived.

Daddy Springy told him to move to the inside of the car, other side of Poorly Boy where there was lots of room next to him, Mum being in the front next to Dad. Crumble Bee refused. His eyes were bad and it was too dark further inside. His eyes would be strained and start to water.

'But it's still lighter in the car than in the shed,' said Daddy Springy.

'Yes but the shed's not moving,' moaned the bee.

The original logic of this prompted Mum to ask if the bee could be shut up in a not too drastic way as he was making her feel less than excited than she'd like.

'Don't you worry Mummy, Daddy Springy knows what's wrong. Give us the lotion.'

'No use arguing, Mum,' said Dad wearily, though she did all the while she rummaged for the suntan lotion in the bag with personal items, plus, Poorly Boy's heart tablets, Dad's stomach tablets and her special travel mints, (the ones that soothed her nerves on journeys just like this one).

Naturally always right, by the time they'd got the car parked, (at least 300 yards from the sea front), Daddy Springy was explaining how he'd concluded Crumble Bee had sun burn.

'Blisters,' offered Poorly Boy in support of the rabbit's lecture.

'You can tell when the ear blisters.' This, being far less long winded than the rabbit's medical-type-none-medical-terminology. Both Mum and Dad were feeling excitement ebb from them as the Sandhill Tide ebbed. Dad was also worrying how much the long scratch, down the side of his car, (fault of course of that other car), was going to cost him. Mum was fed up and irritated with her husband and the big headed rabbit, the small minded bee, and by no means least, Poorly Boy and his big imagination. Herself as well for forgetting to bring those so necessary mints.

Things improved when at last they saw the beach. At least hope renewed. They located a spot of bodiless sand underneath the rusty pier, well out of the sun, which suited Crumble Bee no end.

The moment of relief soon over Dad and Poorly Boy rapidly vanished from sight down a deep hole. Daddy Springy sat by Mum becoming sandier and sandier as the one and a half diggers showered it over them. It was all very exciting, especially after the hole had been dug when they straight away filled it in again as neither of the diggers could find any use for it.

Sandwiches were exciting and the sandy grit filled ones tasted particularly good, so much so that the unexpectedly happy Crumble Bee was given them all to eat after expressing his great liking for them. Mum's tan was definitely postponed as dark clouds now began to drop rusty rain upon their heads from the pier beams above.

But the sea front cafe was, however, genuinely exciting. Dad got into an argument with Mum who'd forgotten to bring his stomach tablets from the car. Daddy Springy got into an argument with Crumble Bee, (most unexpectedly as well), about the rabbit's envisaged extension to Garden Shed Infirmary. These would provide Nurse Nelly with, 'A proper clinic for dealing with problems like clipping toe nails on stuffed Koala bears.' (Poorly Boy had been struck by the large claws on the feet of a soft-toy Koala in a shop, and his inventive mind had wondered how he might deal with such feet in the event of soft toys being admitted for similar minor necessities. Not just nail cutting, but ear wax getting outs and broken stitches the team had to sort out when Mum wouldn't). Crumble Bee objected strongly, regardless of the sandwiches, to proposals meaning he'd lose overall control of any part of hospital management.

Both arguments continued on and off throughout fish and chips, when it stopped raining for a while, and though Daddy Springy and Crumble Bee agreed to put the matter up for vote amongst the staff, (meaning Baby Kenneth would vote alone as he was the only member without a direct interest - in much of anything as it happened), Mum and Dad didn't agree to agree to anything whatsoever. The stomach tablet issue was hotly contested.

'You've a pocket Ben when all's said and done. Why leave it all to me?' And that business of the scratch on the car also began to come back again for a nose in.

'You weren't looking Sue. You weren't even on the side it happened so I should know.'

When Poorly Boy couldn't leave without fetching some 'poorly empty shells to find something to put in at home, save them being lonely' - that was it for Mum who went back to the car in a huff. A rather downcast Dad spent the next one and a half hour putting a motley collection of shells into a carrier bag.

'Aren't we glad, Dad, Crumble Bee's not been the pain we all expected?' enthused an exultant Poorly Boy.

'He's not grumbled hardly at all since we arrived and he's been reasonable over the hospital thing. It's Mum's been the most grumbly of the four of us.'

Dad maintained a strained silence.

As he stood with the final shell in his hand there came a touch on his arm followed by softly spoken words,

'Ben I've lost the car.' To see her again brought his first smile all afternoon - though fleetingly. The first excitement since the cafe was now upon them as they chased off across the sands towards the town upon Dad's cry of

'Follow me, this way.' A brief smile of relief at her touch - and the dawning of realisation that the car might have been stolen, scratch and all.

Poorly Boy enjoyed such events no end as he got to ride on Dad's shoulders at a real fast pace. Mum followed on as best she could, carrying bag, bucket and spades, helped by Crumble Bee and Daddy Springy.

Baby Kenneth had the casting vote; being the only voter. Quite unexpectedly, he voted for Crumble Bee, so the proposed clinic was deferred for now. Nelly had fallen out with the baby rabbit over the Hampton Court Maze, Poorly Boy learnt after arrival home that night. He didn't ask why and wasn't bothered being far too tired to build a clinic tomorrow anyway.

Lying happily in his bed, he looked back on his day at Sandhill On The Rocks. The door opened and Mum came in to kiss him goodnight. As she turned to leave she began to chuckle.

'Oh Poorly Boy I'll never forget Dad's face, will you?' I'm pleased he saw the funny side of my forgetting where the car was, and going to the wrong car park all together!'

'Yes Mum I nearly rolled off his shoulders when he broke up laughing. Everybody thought we'd gone mad!'

'To sleep now, sweetheart,' Dad stood framed in the doorway by the passage light.

'Dad can we find an ants' nest tomorrow?'

'Whatever for?'

'So as ants can run about those seashells. That way they'll have company all the time, just like when they had little fishes in them.'

'I know just the place,' smiled Dad.

'I'm too tired to build a clinic, Dad. That's why Baby Kenneth voted against it for now.'

'Yes Son. He must be growing up to make such important decisions,' yawned Dad.

'Night, night, Dad.'

Daddy Springy and all the toys snuggled around Poorly Boy. As he drifted off to sleep, he was sure he heard Crumble Bee out in the shed singing a little song, come softly through his bedroom window. Crumble Bee, as Dad had hoped all those hours ago, had had a truly exciting day.

'Just like my Dad, always thinking of others.' Poorly Boy was asleep.

SWEET REMEMBRANCE
Betty M Irwin-Burton

Candyfloss clouds were the only interruption in the bright blue sky. Beneath them was the hustle and bustle of everyday life carrying on regardless. People always found a way of ignoring the bad things that were happening and sometimes the good things as well. The city was buzzing; it was a bank holiday. Practically everybody had the day off work. The children dragged their parents around the shops trying to squeeze extra gifts out of them, and the elderly took time to sit on park benches and let the breeze blow them down memory lane. It was a day when anything could happen and anything was possible.

Felicity turned the old key over in her hand. This was positively the last chance she had of finding a suitable house for herself.

The studio flat was too expensive and not her 'type' of dwelling place, and the modern terraced house was definitely more suited to the young couples living in that area.

Slowly and almost hesitantly, she turned the corner and walked towards number 13, an old Edwardian villa. It was sadly in need of paint, and some repairs to windows and door, but not unattractive for all that.

Mr Danver of 'Danver, Danver and Hoddly' the estate agents had admitted it had been on their books for quite some time.

'It's a little run down and in need of a lick of paint,' he's said lamely, but Felicity thought it was more likely to be the house number that put people off: 13 was unpopular.

She put the key in the lock and it turned smoothly and the door swung open. The air was musty and she hurried to open the door on the far right at the end of the hall.

She was instantly swathed in sunlight. It filled the room, and the heady, sweet perfume of old English roses and white flocks floated through the broken windowpane in the French windows. A feeling of warmth and love enveloped her, and seeing an old rocking chair by the windows she slowly sank onto its cobwebbed seat and rocked herself gently.

The heavily perfumed air and warm sunlight relaxed her, and her eyelids felt heavy and closed involuntarily.

She drifted off; but soon the deep drone of aero-engines caused her to stir, and as she looked up her eye caught the glint from a mirror on the fireplace wall.

As she looked - a face was reflected in it. She stared in fascination. A young airforce officer was combing back his hair. He wore the insignia of a pilot officer of the last war. Felicity gripped the arms of the chair until her knuckles turned white, and a sharp tingling ran down her spine. Her breath escaped in painful gasps as her heart now beat rapidly and a crushing weight seemed to bear down upon her. The sound was apparently heard by the young airman for he turned and looked at her.

'Flissy!' She recognised the rich, deep voice, and the warm, brown eyes that met hers.

'Robert . . .?' Her own voice faltered with shock and emotion. It couldn't be! Her mind was in a turmoil. Why, it was over fifty years since she had last seen Robert! Fifty-eight to be exact since that day when his plane failed to return from the big raid on Germany. She had been a golden-haired, blue-eyed, eighteen year-old, and he a dark haired, tall, young pilot with the chiselled features of a Greek god. They had been engaged to be married quite soon. She closed her eyes and rubbed them with her handkerchief, but as she opened them again he was standing in front of her, and strong hands pulled her out of the rocking chair.

'Darling Flissy,' he murmured, and drew her into his arms. She recognised the clean, masculine smell of him; the expensive aftershave he used and the tweedy scent of his uniform. Her muddled mind tried to make sense of this thing. She may have retained much of her good looks and golden hair, but she was no longer a girl. She was an elderly woman with shadows beneath her eyes; but, strangely Robert saw nothing of this. He actually seemed to see her as he once knew her!

'It's been so long! Oh darling Robert!' she whispered and her hands reached up to his broad shoulders and held him close. Oh, the dear, nearness of him. The warm strength she could clearly feel through the uniform he wore.

Gently stroking her hair, he spoke again. 'I came back for you Felicity my love.'

She felt very tired and the joy of his nearness almost stopped her hammering heart. Robert was safe. He held her in his arms. It had been so long, and so lonely. A small sob reached her throat, but was never released.

Moonlight now flooded the room as George Danvers walked through the doorway and shone his torch around the place. He then saw her in the rocking chair. Her head had fallen back in an awkward position. 'Miss Campian!' He sprinted forward but as he touched her wrist - it was cold and lifeless. Her fingers clasped something, and as he dropped her wrist a gilded airforce badge fell from the lifeless grasp. It had something engraved on it. 'Pilot Officer Greyshaw', and a date - 1943. A feeling like cold water flooded down George Danvers back. 'Oh God!' he shuddered. Quickly he struggled with his mobile phone and minutes later the paramedics were gently, but swiftly easing Felicity into the ambulance with a sorry look at George Danvers. They confirmed that it was far too late to attempt any kind of resuscitation.

George followed them in his car. Looking at his watch he saw it was 10 o'clock and she must have been there since around 4.00pm. He had only gone there on pure chance as he thought she must surely have returned to her flat to mull it over before deciding. She must have had a sudden, colossal heart attack, he thought. After all, young as she looked - she must have been in her seventies. I wonder where she got that Airforce badge from, he pondered? The last occupant had been a very old, retired professor of mathematics and the house had been empty for 14 months now. All the furniture, barring an old rocker and a mildewed mirror, had long since been removed.

A niece, on turning out Felicity's personal things had found three photographs tucked under a letter in an old shoe box. One was of a seventeen year-old Felicity lying on a grassy riverbank with a laughing young man sitting tickling her nose with a buttercup. Another showed the two dancing in a ballroom decorated with Christmas hangings and the third was a close-up head and shoulders of a handsome young pilot officer, and there, glittering over a breast pocket was a beautiful Airforce badge, engraved - Pilot Officer Greyshaw - 1943.

Emma, the niece, looked at the badge in her hand. It was, without doubt, identical. How in the world had it come into her aunt's hand in a strange house, and over 50 years of time?

HIS PHANTOM LOVE
Vera Parsonage

*Candyfloss clouds were the only interruption in the bright blue sky.
Beneath them was the hustle and bustle of everyday life carrying on
regardless. People always found a way of ignoring the bad things that
were happening and sometimes the good things as well. The city was
buzzing; it was a bank holiday. Practically everybody had the day off
work. The children dragged their parents around the shops trying to
squeeze extra gifts out of them, and the elderly took time to sit on park
benches and let the breeze blow them down memory lane. It was a day
when anything could happen and anything was possible.*

For Danny bank holiday was his busiest time; he had been out since
the crack of dawn sitting in the taxi rank outside the park, and watching
the world go by. He had hardly time to light a cigarette and was kept
busy ferrying passengers to their destinations. Tired mothers with noisy
children, shoppers loaded with parcels - anything could happen for
Danny on a bank holiday and he was ready to face whatever came
along. More than once he had thrown a drunk out of his cab.

By four o'clock it was time for his break and a strong cup of tea. He
had hardly time to relax when in walked an attractive young lady.
Danny couldn't believe his luck when she came over to his table and sat
on the seat opposite him. He wasn't slow at pulling the birds. His mates
would tease him, but, girls were to him a good night out. This girl
seemed different, there was an old-fashioned look about her, not like
most of the girls he had known. Her dress was neat but not trendy, and
her hair fell in ringlets around a lace collar. Danny had never seen any
girl so pretty, her smile was enchanting.

'I need help,' she said. 'My car has broken down, and it's too far to
walk home and Mother will be worried if I'm late. Could you take me
in your taxi?'

'I'll do more than that, I'll take a look at it for you,' he said.

'It's outside the park gates,' was her answer.

'Come on,' said Danny putting down his cup, and taking her arm,
they walked outside.

Sitting besides him in the taxi there was a sweet smell of lavender, a
strange smell of perfume for a girl in this modern age. It was unlike the
perfume his past lady friends wore.

The car was parked on some wasteland outside the park. Danny got out of his taxi and walked across to it. He gasped with surprise, it was the oldest car he had ever seen. It was like the one in the old photographs that Grandad had in the early 1940's. It shone like a new car and he doubted if any of his tools would be suitable to do any sort of repair. Fortunately there wasn't much wrong with it, and Danny soon had the engine working. He opened the door and slid inside. The seating was immaculate. Turning on the engine, he heard that it sounded perfect. It was his gain that she thought her car had a fault or he may never have met her. Fate had brought them together and he would make the most of it.

When his taxi was not in use he would bring out his motorcycle and career down the street and out into the country. Biking was his hobby. It was a new venture for Jane, she loved hanging on to him on the back of the bike. Life changed for him, he gave up flirting with other girls and he knew he was in love with her. Jane was different from any girl he had known - the best good thing that had happened to him.

They had been together a few months when he asked her to marry him. In her heart she knew this could never be. For a second, she lost her smile, and there were tears in her eyes. For one frightening moment, Danny wondered if she was already married, but this couldn't be true, she loved him so much. He never asked her again - the joy of being together was enough to satisfy his feelings.

He lived in a small bedsit and on winter nights they would cuddle together by the fire and listen to the radio. Some nights he would be called out and his taxi would be in motion for hours. On his return Jane would have his supper ready. She would never take him home to meet her mother - maybe she wouldn't approve of her daughter marrying a common taxi driver.

It had been a busy day, bank holidays were always busy. Danny was remembering the last one when he had met Jane. It had been a long evening and it was late when he got home. Finding no light on he walked into the flat and there was no sign of Jane, no explanation for her absence, Jane had gone forever.

The weeks passed and the months, the loneliness was unbearable. Next Sunday he would take a day off and try to find her. He would find her home, as he had to know why she had left him. She had also left some of her belongings in the bedsit. Inside an empty purse he found an address. Danny decided to go there and hopefully locate her. His searching took him out of town. Rock Cottage was on the end of a row of cottages tucked away in a cul-de-sac. His heart was beating as he walked up the path and knocked on the door. He saw a curtain move.

Eventually the door was opened by a sweet old lady, so like Jane that she had to be her mother. 'Could I speak to Jane please?' he asked. The old lady gave him a sad smile and took his arm, leading him into the cottage. Danny shivered, he felt that Jane wasn't there in that neat little cottage. On the wall was a framed picture smiling at him, a smile so familiar, her beautiful hair falling in ringlets onto a lace collar.

The old lady spoke quietly. 'I lost her twenty years ago. I believe she had a taxi driver friend but she never brought him home to meet me. I know they were very much in love and they would go riding on his motorbike. That's him,' she pointed to a photograph of them both on the mantelshelf, they were sitting together on the bike. The old lady rambled on, 'He was not unlike you. They were talking of getting married but she never brought him home to meet me. One Sunday afternoon they were on their way here I believe, when they swerved to avoid a child crossing the road and crashed into a wall and they were both killed. If only I had met him!'

'You have, dear Mother, you have,' he turned and kissed her as he left to go.

It was almost dark on the rank. Danny shivered, and lit a cigarette, I must have been asleep he thought. It had been a while since he had been in the café, and talked to the lovely girl. Where did she go? It had been a strange bank holiday, most of the people had left the park. He looked at his watch, 'It's time I went home. I've worked too hard,' he muttered to himself.

As he put the key in the latch something touched his cheek, it was like the wing of a butterfly and in the night air, he smelled the sweet scent of lavender. 'Goodnight dear Jane,' he whispered. 'Wherever you are, goodnight.'

AUGUST 2001 - A TRUE STORY!
Bill Baker

*Candyfloss clouds were the only interruption in the bright blue sky.
Beneath them was the hustle and bustle of everyday life carrying on
regardless. People always found a way of ignoring the bad things that
were happening and sometimes the good things as well. The city was
buzzing; it was a bank holiday. Practically everybody had the day off
work. The children dragged their parents around the shops trying to
squeeze extra gifts out of them, and the elderly took time to sit on park
benches and let the breeze blow them down memory lane. It was a day
when anything could happen and anything was possible.*

Eighty-one year-old Bill Baker was enjoying life in the garden. Clad
only in T-shirt and shorts, he pottered about pulling a weed up here and
nipping the dead heads of his pansies there. He was musing to himself
that there was always something to do in the garden whatever time of
the year it happened to be.

Of course, Bill didn't consider it a chore. To him, gardening was the
second best thing in life. The first was, of course, his writing. To sit at
his computer and let his brain take over and the stories literally flowed
out. What more could a bloke want? His mind came back to his garden.
He'd pick some runner beans for his lunch. They were hanging in great
bunches and his mouth watered at the thought of them piled on his plate
with a great knob of butter melting over them.

He picked a good half pound and took them into the kitchen with the
intention of preparing them for lunch, when suddenly a queer sort of
feeling occurred in his head. In that split second he knew that it was a
stroke, though he had never come across one before. He went into the
living room and phoned the doctor, who took his name and address and
the address and phone number of his son, and told Bill to sit down and
leave the rest to him. That was the last thing Bill remembered.

The story is taken up by his children.

Hello! My name is Keith and my wife's Cathie, and when the doctor
phoned us we set off for Dad's in our car, a distance of three miles, and
reached there in about ten minutes. Luckily I had the keys to his front
door, and went straight in to find Dad unconscious in a chair with his
trousers half on and his shorts on the floor beside him. The next

moment the ambulance arrived and the medics took over, loading him into the ambulance with great difficulty, as Dad weighed a good seventeen stone or more.

On reaching hospital the staff there took over and we could only wait until eventually a doctor came and told us what was being done. Medically, nothing! He explained that he could only ensure that Dad was kept clean and warm and fed, and let nature take its course.

Later that night, Dad's daughter Sian turned up. She and David her husband had taken their two children to London and had only just got back to Swansea. I told her what had happened and said that nothing else could be done that wasn't already being done. We visited Dad daily and were joined by Mike, another son who lived in Haverfordwest, and eventually Dad opened his eyes and said, 'Hello, you lot. What's going on?' and promptly fell asleep again. This sort of thing went on for seven weeks until finally Dad regained consciousness and discovered that the whole of his right side was paralysed.

Bill takes up the story again:

It was then that Bill realised just how much work the hospital staff did. They had to do every little thing for him, even to wiping his bottom as he lay there day after day. Nothing was too much trouble for those angels in blue. Then came the big day in Bill's life. Two lady physiotherapists descended upon him and told him he'd been stuck in bed for far too long, and it was time to get up again. They pushed his bedclothes back and got him sat on the edge of the bed, and then, with one on either side of him, they told him to get up. After a couple of agonising minutes that seemed like hours, Bill found himself standing by the bed supported by the two girls.

The response from the whole ward was terrific! Everyone clapped and cheered. There was no doubt about it, Bill was a very popular patient. He gave a very lopsided grin to the whole ward and collapsed back onto the bed.

Then followed a period of hard-going for Bill. It seemed that those physiotherapists never left him alone. All he wanted to do was to go to sleep, and they wouldn't let him. They punched him and pummelled him and did everything they could to keep him going. So, slowly but surely, Bill took the road to recovery. With the aid of a Zimmer frame, he learned to walk again. What was the hardest part of his recovery however, was his speech. He just couldn't get things out. How people put up with him, he just didn't know! What made sense to him came out as a string of gibberish to other people. However, he persevered, and slowly, so *bloody* slowly, he was winning!

Then came the magical day. Bill was going home! He had lost five months of his life, and he could only walk with two sticks, but he was *going home*.

It didn't matter that he lived alone. His kids were only a telephone call away. His two cats had been cared for and showed their love for him. He hobbled around the house and garden which he never expected to ever see again. It was wonderful!

That hot and humid day that had begun so well was now far away in the memories of time. In a day or two it would be Christmas! And he was *alive*!

THE PARK BENCH
Tony MacMillan

Candyfloss clouds were the only interruption in the bright blue sky. Beneath them was the hustle and bustle of everyday life carrying on regardless. People always found a way of ignoring the bad things that were happening and sometimes the good things as well. The city was buzzing; it was a bank holiday. Practically everybody had the day off work. The children dragged their parents around the shops trying to squeeze extra gifts out of them, and the elderly took time to sit on park benches and let the breeze blow them down memory lane. It was a day when anything could happen and anything was possible.

Memory lane took me to last year's bank holiday. The day was as hot then and, as usual, the park was as full of children playing happily and noisily.

That had been the day when I moved to a different seat in the park and had first become away of the boy. I noticed him particularly because he was standing apart from the others, who were playing so happily. It was as if he were in a little oasis of stillness and quiet, whilst all around him there was movement and noise. Strange how play always seems to require noise, but I suppose it was the same when I was young.

I should perhaps explain why I moved my seat. I could have seen the playing children perfectly well from where I sat before, but I knew that an elderly man watching children regularly from the same seat would have become a figure of suspicion. How things have changed from the carefree days of my youth. All we had to worry about then were sirens and bombs.

Many times when my friends and I played in the park, we were watched by lonely old gentlemen and I cannot recall any of us coming to any harm. It was handy to have someone to kick our balls back. Now I am an elderly gentleman myself and I have to worry how a suspicious world sees me. Part pity and part fear.

However I should also explain why I am in the park at all. Since my wife died I have found myself with plenty of spare time and nothing to fill it.

There were, of course, household chores but as my wife had been ill for some time, I was used to doing them and you can only clean a flat so much. So I had time on my hands and I took to walking in the park.

There were other elderly men like myself of course, but I had never been a very sociable person and I found great difficulty in starting conversations with strangers. It was for that reason I usually sat by myself.

I soon fell into the habit of watching the children playing. They looked so young and happy, and they laughed and played with no inhibitions. I suppose they reminded me of my youth.

I liked to see them because my wife and I never had any family. Even when she was young there was something the matter with my wife's insides but I never did know what it was. However we made a good life in spite of that and we never mentioned that we wanted children. But I know that she did. And so did I. Perhaps that was the main reason I liked to watch them play. But I was very careful not to speak to any of them.

I think it was because of my wife's illness that I never did have the time for any hobbies and it was now far too late to learn. So in the summer it was the park and isolation.

Over the days and weeks that followed my change of seat, I found myself watching this one lonely boy I had become aware of. He was a quiet fair-headed little boy - about six, I guessed. He looked wistful and I longed for one of the other children to speak to him, but they all ignored him. As time went by I began to be quite annoyed at the fact that they left him so alone. If I could see that he wanted to join in, why couldn't they? I so wanted to interfere but I knew that I shouldn't.

He was clean and neat in a bright yellow shirt. I thought his mother must take good care of him, he was obviously loved. But I never saw him with a grown-up. Day after day he just stood to one side of the others, a ball under his arm, watching them. Lonely, like me.

One day in high summer, I was surprised to come to my lonely seat, to find a young woman sitting there. Nobody else had sat on my bench for months. I nodded to her and sat at the other end to watch the sun shining on the grass and the children playing. We sat in silence for several minutes.

'Do you come here often?'

I jumped and turned to her. It was the first time anybody had spoken to me for ages. 'Yes. I come here every day. I like it.'

'Yes. I like it too.' She smiled, but it was a sad smile.

'I like to watch the children play,' I confessed.

She said nothing and that made me a little nervous. I wondered if I had said something wrong. It made me chatter. I told her about the little boy who never joined in with the others and I turned to point him out but, for once, he wasn't there.

'I used to have a little boy,' she said. 'He played here. I used to leave him with the others. They said they would look after him. I would leave him here for about half an hour, then I would come back for him. But one day I got talking to another mother and I was away longer than usual. Only about five minutes. He must have gone to look for me. He went to the edge of the road and stopped because he knew he was not meant to go any further. But just then a ball was kicked past him and he ran after it. The driver had no chance. This is the first time I've been back in over a year.'

'I'm sorry.'

'Where's your lonely little boy?' and she turned to look across the park.

I looked too but, surprisingly, he still wasn't there. 'I can't see him today.'

She sat looking intently. 'What's he like?'

'Nice looking lad. Fair-haired. About six, I guess. He always wears a bright yellow shirt. So neat and clean.'

The silence that followed made me turn to look at her. I saw her eyes fill with tears and getting up, she walked away. Then it occurred to me that perhaps this time he had waited for his mother.

Over the months that followed I looked often, but I never saw the little boy again.